ATTITUDE

AND OTHER STORIES

LINDA NAGATA

Mythic Island Press LLC
Kula, Hawaii

First Electronic Edition July 2022
First Print Edition July 2022

PUBLISHING HISTORY:

Codename: Delphi Copyright © 2014 by Linda Nagata.
First published in *Lightspeed Magazine*, April 2014

Nightside On Callisto Copyright © 2012 by Linda Nagata.
First published in *Lightspeed Magazine*, May 2012

Attitude Copyright © 2014 by Linda Nagata.
First published in *Reach For Infinity*, May 2014

Devil in the Dust Copyright © 2019 by Linda Nagata.
First published in *Mission Critical*, July 2019

Region Five Copyright © 2017 by Linda Nagata.
First published in *Infinite Stars*, October 2017

The Way Home Copyright © 2015 by Linda Nagata.
First published in *Operation Arcana*, March 2015

The Last Good Man (excerpt) Copyright © 2017 by Linda Nagata.

Cover design by Emily Irwin
Cover photo by Benjamin Suter from Pexels

Mythic Island Press LLC
PO Box 1293
Kula, HI 96790-1293
MythicIslandPress.com

ATTITUDE

AND OTHER STORIES

CONTENTS

Codename: Delphi

"VALDEZ, YOU NEED to slow down," Karin Larsen warned, each syllable crisply pronounced into a mic. "Stay behind the seekers. If you overrun them, you're going to walk into a booby trap."

Five thousand miles away from Karin's control station, Second Lieutenant Valdez was jacked up on adrenaline and in a defiant mood. "*Negative!*" she said, her voice arriving over Karin's headphones. "*Delphi, we've got personnel down and need to move fast. This route scans clear. I am not waiting for the seekers to clear it again.*"

The battleground was an ancient desert city. Beginning at sunset, firefights had flared up all across its tangled neighborhoods and Valdez was right that her squad needed to advance—but not so fast that they ran into a trap.

"The route is *not* clear," Karin insisted. "The last overflight to scan this alley was forty minutes ago. Anything could have happened since then."

Karin's worksite was an elevated chair within a little room inside a secure building. She faced a curved monitor a meter-and-a-half high, set an easy reach away. Windows checkered its screen, grouped by color-codes representing different clients. The windows could slide, change sequence, and overlap, but they could never completely hide one another; the system wouldn't allow it. This was Karin's interface to the war.

Presently centered onscreen were two gold-rimmed windows, each displaying a video feed captured by an aerial seeker: palm-sized drones equipped with camera eyes, audio pickups, and chemical sensors. The seekers flew ahead of Valdez and her urban infantry squad, one at eye level and the other at an elevation of six meters, scouting a route between brick-and-stucco tenements. They flew too slowly for Valdez.

The lieutenant was out of sight of the seekers' camera eyes, but Karin could hear the soft patter of her boot plates as she advanced at a hurried trot, and the tread of the rest of the squad trailing behind her. Echoing off the buildings, there came the pepper of distant rifle fire and a heavier caliber weapon answering.

Onscreen, positioned above the two video feeds, was a third window that held the squad map—a display actively tracking the position and status of each soldier.

Outfitted in bullet-proof vests and rigged in the titanium struts of light-infantry exoskeletons—"armor and bones"—the squad advanced through the alley at a mandated ten-meter interval, a regulation that reduced the odds of multiple casualties if they encountered an IED or a grenade. Only Lieutenant Valdez failed to maintain the proper distance, crowding within two meters of the seekers in her rush to answer the call for backup.

"Valdez, this is not a simple firefight. It's a widespread, well-planned insurgent offensive. Every kid with a grudge—"

"No lectures, Delphi. Just get these seekers moving faster."

Any faster, and the little drones could miss something critical.

Local time was past midnight and no lights shone in the alley, but in nightvision the walls of the buildings and the trash-strewn brick pavement gleamed in crisp, green detail. Karin wasn't the only one monitoring the seekers' feeds; a battle AI watched them too. It generated an ongoing report, displayed alongside the windows. She glanced at it and saw an alert for trace scents of explosives—but with a battle in progress that didn't mean anything. Otherwise the report was good: no suspicious heat signatures or whispering voices or inexplicable motion within the apartments.

Her gaze shifted back to the video feed. A faint gleam caught her attention; a hair-thin line close to the ground that justified her caution. "Tripwire," she announced. She reached out to the screen; dragged her finger across the line. The gesture created a fleeting highlight on the display screen of Valdez's visor, clearly marking the tripwire's position. "Six meters ahead."

"*Shit*." Valdez pulled up sharply. A faint background tone sounded as she switched her audio to gen-com. "*Tripwire*," she said, addressing her squad. "*Move back*."

The tone dropped out, and Valdez was talking again solely to Karin. "*Ambush?*"

"Searching." It was a good bet someone was monitoring the tripwire.

A set of windows bordered in blue glided to the center of Karin's screen: Lieutenant Deng's color code. The insurgent offensive had erupted all along the northern border, striking hard at Deng's rural district. At approximately 2200 she'd been lured into an ambush. The resulting firefight had left one of her soldiers seriously wounded.

Distance did not mute the impatience—or the frustration—in Deng's voice as she spoke over the headphones, "*Delphi, where's my medevac helicopter?*"

On nights like this, a big part of Karin's job was triage. Deng's situation was no longer "hot." The insurgents had fled, and the helicopter had already been requested. Determining an ETA would not get it there faster. So she told Deng, "Stand by."

Then she swiped the blue windows out of the way and returned her attention to the feeds from the seekers, directing one to fly higher. The angle of view shifted, and Karin spied a figure crouched on the sloping, clay-tiled roof of a low building not far ahead. She drew a highlight around it. "Valdez, see that?"

A glance at the squad map showed that Valdez had retreated a few meters from the tripwire. One specialist remained with her, while the rest of the squad had dropped back under the supervision of a sergeant.

"*I see him*," Valdez said. "*Target confirmed?*"

"Negative. Twenty seconds."

Karin sent a seeker buzzing toward the figure on the rooftop and then she switched her focus back to Deng's blue-coded windows, fanning them open so she could see the one that tracked the status of the medevac helicopter. The offensive was unprecedented and air support was in high demand. Deng's wounded soldier was third on the list for pickup. "Deng, ETA on the medevac is forty-plus minutes," Karin warned; that was assuming the helicopter stayed in the air. She slid the blue windows away again, switching back to Valdez.

Wind soughing between the buildings veiled the soft buzz of the seeker so that the figure on the roof didn't hear it coming. Details emerged as the little drone got closer. One of those details was a rifle—aimed at Valdez. "Target confirmed," Karin said without hesitation. "Shoot to kill."

Valdez was watching the same feed. "*That's a kid!*"

It *was* a kid. The battle AI estimated a male, fourteen years old. It didn't matter. The boy was targeting Valdez and that made him the enemy.

"Take the shot."

The boy fired first. He missed, but he squeezed the trigger again. His second shot caught Valdez in the shoulder, spinning her into the wall. "*Fuck.*"

"Valdez, get down!"

The lieutenant dropped to a crouch. The specialist was already hunkered down behind her. He aimed over her shoulder and shot—but too late. The kid had opened a roof-access door, retreating inside the building.

Karin checked Valdez's biometrics: high stress, but no indication that the slug had penetrated. Her armor had protected her.

"A biometric ID on the shooter is in the system," Karin told her. "You can hunt him down later."

"*Right. I'm going to drop back, rejoin the squad, and go around.*"

While Valdez reorganized, Karin switched to her third client, Lieutenant Holder. The set of windows monitoring his squad was coded orange. Holder was assigned to a district just outside the city. Tonight his squad waited in ambush for a suspected small-arms shipment coming in from the west. She checked his status: nominal. Checked the squad: noted all seven soldiers in position on either side of an asphalt road. Checked the wide-field view from the infrared camera on the squad's surveillance drone and noted the suspect truck, still at almost five kilometers away.

There was time.

Karin sighed, took a sip of chilled water from a bottle stashed in a pouch at the side of her chair, and for just a moment she squeezed her dry eyes shut. She'd already been six hours on-shift, with only one ten-minute break and that was two hours ago. There would be hours more before she could rest. Most shifts went on until her clients were out of harm's way—that's just how it was, how it needed to be. She'd learned that early.

Karin had trained as a handler for the usual reason: money. She'd needed to pay off a student loan. Two years so far, with a fat savings account to show for it. The money was good, no argument, but the lifestyle? Some handlers joked that the job was like a video game—one so intense it left you shaking and exhausted at the end of every shift—but for her it had never been a game. The lives she handled were real. Slip up, and she could put a soldier in the grave. That was her nightmare. She'd had soldiers grievously wounded, but so far none had died on her shift. Lately, she'd started thinking that maybe she should quit before it happened. On a night like tonight, that thought was close to the surface.

The blue windows slid to center again. Karin popped the bottle back into its pouch as an irate Deng spoke through her headphones. *"Delphi, I can't wait forty minutes for the medevac. I've got six enemy at-large. They have their own wounded to worry about, but once they get organized, they're going to move on the settlement. If we don't get there first, there are going to be reprisals. I need approval from Command to split the squad."*

"Stand by."

Karin captured a voice clip of Deng's request and sent it to the Command queue, flagged highest priority. But before she could slide the blue windows aside, someone opened an emergency channel—an act that overrode the communications of every handler on-shift. *"I need support!"* a shrill voice yelled through Karin's headphones. She flinched back, even as she recognized Sarno, another handler. The panic in his voice told her that he had made a mistake. A critical mistake, maybe a fatal one. *"I need support! Now. I just can't—"*

His transmission cut out. The shift supervisor's voice came on—calm, crisp, alert: the way handlers were trained to speak. *"I'm on it."*

Karin's hands shook. Sarno worked a chair just a few doors down from her. He was new, and new handlers sometimes got overwhelmed, but panic was always the wrong response. At the end of the shift, every handler got to go home, smoke a joint, collapse in a bed with soft sheets, get laid if they wanted to. Their clients didn't have that option. Sarno needed to remember that. Sarno needed to remember that however rough it got in the control room, no one was trying to end *his* life.

Right now the supervisor would be assisting him, coaching him, getting him back on track. Karin refocused, striving to put the incident out of her mind.

Dragging the gold-rimmed windows to center, she checked on Valdez, confirming the lieutenant had safely exited the alley. There were no alerts from the battle AI, so Karin switched to Deng's window-set. Rigged in armor and bones, the squad had formed a perimeter to protect their wounded soldier. Around them, dry grass rustled beneath spindly trees, and the stars glowed green in nightvision. Karin switched to Holder. He was still hunkered down with his squad alongside the road. An infrared feed from Holder's surveillance drone showed the target vehicle only a klick-and-a-half away, approaching fast without headlights.

Just as Karin brought her attention back to Valdez, the shift supervisor spoke.

"Karin, we've got an emergency situation. I need to transfer another client to you."

"No way, Michael."

"Karin—"

"No. I've got three active operations and I can barely stay on top of them. If you give me one more client, I'm going to resign."

"Fine, Karin! Resign. But just finish this shift first. I need you. Sarno walked. He fucking walked out and left his clients."

Sarno walked? Karin lost track of her windows as she tried to make sense of it. How could he walk out? What they did here was not a video game. There was no pause button on this war. Every handler was responsible for the lives of real people.

Michael took her hesitation as agreement. *"I'm splitting the load. You only have to take one. Incoming now."*

Her throat aching, she took another sip of water, a three-second interval when her mind could rove . . . this time back to the kick-boxing session that started her day, every day: a fierce routine that involved every muscle—*strike, strike, strike*—defiantly physical, because a handler had to be in top form to do this kind of work, and Karin hated to make mistakes.

As she looked up again, a glowing green dot expanded into a new set of windows, with the client's bio floating to the top. Shelley, James. A lieutenant with a stellar field rating. *Good*, Karin thought. *Less work for me.*

As she fanned the windows, the live feed opened with the triple concussion of three grenades going off one after another. She bit down on her lip, anxious to engage, but she needed an overview of the situation first. Locating the squad map, she scanned the terrain and the positions of each soldier. There were five personnel besides Shelley: a sergeant, two specialists, and two privates. The map also showed the enemy's positions and their weaponry—field intelligence automatically compiled from helmet cams and the squad's surveillance drone.

The map showed that Shelley's squad was outnumbered and outgunned.

With little shelter in a flat rural landscape of dusty red-dirt pastures and drought-stricken tree farms, they protected themselves by continuously shifting position in a fight to hold a defensive line north of the village that was surely the target of this raid. The insurgents' ATVs had already been eliminated, but two pickup trucks remained, one rigged with a heavy machine gun and the other with a rocket-launcher pod, probably stripped off a downed helicopter. The rockets it used would have a range to four kilometers. Shelley needed to take the rocket-launcher out before it targeted the village and before his squad burned through their inventory of grenades.

The sound of the firefight dropped out as her get-acquainted session was overridden by Deng's windows sliding to the center. A communication had come in from Command. Deng's request to split the squad had been approved. Karin forwarded the order, following up with a verbal link. "Deng, your request has been approved. Orders specify two personnel remain with the wounded; four proceed to the settlement."

"*Thanks, Delphi.*"

Karin switched to Holder. His ambush would go off in seconds. She did a quick scan of the terrain around him, located no additional threats, and then switched focus to Valdez. Cities were the worst. Too many places for snipers to hide. Too many alleys to booby trap. Karin requested an extra surveillance drone to watch the surrounding buildings as Valdez trotted with her squad through the dark streets. She'd feel more secure if she could study the feed from the seekers, but there was no time—because it was her new client who faced the most immediate hazard.

Lieutenant Shelley was on the move, weaving between enemy positions, letting two of his soldiers draw the enemy's attention while he closed on the rocket launcher. The truck that carried the weapon was being backed into the ruins of a still-smoldering, blown-out farmhouse. The roof of the house was gone along with the southern wall, but three stout brick walls remained, thick enough to shelter the rocket crew from enemy fire. Once they had the truck in place, it would be only a minute or two before the bombardment started.

Not a great time to switch handlers.

Karin mentally braced herself, and then she opened a link to Shelley. The sounds of the firefight hammered through her headphones: staccato bursts from assault rifles and then the bone-shaking boom of another grenade launched by the insurgents. A distant, keening scream of agony made her hair stand on end, but a status check showed green so she knew it wasn't one of hers. "Lieutenant Shelley," she said, speaking quickly before he could

protest her intrusion. "My codename is Delphi. You've been transferred to my oversight. I'll be your handler tonight."

His biometrics, already juiced from the ongoing operation,
surged even higher. "*What the Hell?*" he whispered. "*Did you people
get rid of Hawkeye in the middle of an action?*"

"Hawkeye took himself out, Lieutenant."

Karin remembered her earlier assessment of Sarno's break-
down. *He had made a mistake.* What that mistake was, she didn't
know and there was no time to work it out. "I've got an overview
of the situation and I will stay with you."

"*What'd you say your name was?*"

"Delphi."

"*Delphi, you see where I'm going?*"

"Yes."

He scuttled, hunched over to lower his profile, crossing bare
ground between leafless thickets. Shooting was almost constant,
from one side or another, but so far he'd gone unnoticed and none
of it was directed at him.

Karin studied the terrain that remained to be crossed. "You're
going to run out of cover."

"*Understood.*"

A wide swath of open ground that probably served as a pas-
ture in the rainy season lay between Shelley and the shattered
farmhouse. He needed to advance a hundred meters across it to
be within the effective range of his grenade launcher. There were
no defenders in that no-man's-land, but there were at least eight
insurgents sheltering within the remains of the farmhouse—and
the second truck, the one with the machine gun, was just out of
sight on the other side of the ruins.

She fanned the windows just as the lieutenant dropped to his
belly at the edge of the brush. Bringing Shelley's details to the top,
she checked his supplies. "You have two programmable grenades
confirmed inside your weapon. Ten percent of your ammo load
remaining. Lieutenant, that's not enough."

"*It's enough.*"

Karin shook her head. Shelley couldn't see it; it was a gesture meant only for herself. There weren't enough soldiers in his squad to keep him out of trouble once the enemy knew where he was.

Would it be tonight then? she wondered. Would this be the night she lost someone?

"I advise you to retreat."

"*Can't do it, Delphi.*"

It was the expected answer, but she'd had to try.

Nervous tension reduced her to repeating the basics. "Expect them to underestimate how fast you can move and maneuver in your exoskeleton. You can take advantage of that."

The shooting subsided. In the respite, audio pickups caught and enhanced the sound of a tense argument taking place at the distant farmhouse. Then a revving engine overrode the voices.

Karin said, "The other truck, with the machine gun, it's on the move."

"*I see it.*"

A check of his setup confirmed he had the feed from the surveillance drone posted on the periphery of his visor display.

He used gen-com to speak to his squad. "*It's now. Don't let me get killed, okay?*"

They answered, their voices tense, intermingled: "*We got you . . . watch over you . . .*"

Valdez's window-set centered, cutting off their replies. "*Delphi, you there?*"

Her voice was calm, so Karin said, "Stand by," and swiped her window-set aside.

"*. . . kick ass, L. T.*"

Shelley's window-set was still fanned, with the live feed from the surveillance drone on one end of the array. Motion in that window caught Karin's eye, even before the battle AI highlighted it. "Shelley, the machine-gun truck is coming around the north side of the ruins. Everybody on those walls is going to be looking at it."

"*Got it. I'm going.*"

"Negative! Hold your position. On my mark . . ." She identified the soldier positioned a hundred-fifty meters away on Shelley's west flank. Overriding protocol, she opened a link to him, and popped a still image of the truck onto the periphery of his visor. "Hammer it as soon as you have it in sight." The truck fishtailed around the brick walls and Karin told Shelley, "Now."

He took off in giant strides powered by his exoskeleton, zigzagging across the bare ground. There was a shout from the truck, just as the requested assault rifle opened up. The truck's windshield shattered. More covering fire came from the northwest. From the farmhouse voices cried out in fury and alarm. Karin held her breath while Shelley covered another twenty meters and then she told him, "Drop and target!"

He accepted her judgment and slammed to the ground, taking the impact on the arm struts of his exoskeleton as the racing pickup braked in a cloud of dust. Shelley didn't turn to look. The feed from his helmet cams remained fixed on the truck parked between the ruined walls as he set up his shot. The battle AI calculated the angle, and when his weapon was properly aligned, the AI pulled the trigger.

A grenade launched on a low trajectory, transiting the open ground and disappearing under the truck, where it exploded with a deep *whump!*, enfolding the vehicle in a fireball that initiated a thunderous roar of secondary explosions as the rocket propellant ignited. The farmhouse became an incandescent inferno. Nightvision switched off on all devices as white light washed across the open ground.

Karin shifted screens. The feed from the surveillance drone showed a figure still moving in the bed of the surviving truck. An enemy soldier—wounded maybe—but still determined, clawing his way up to the mounted machine gun. "Target to the northwest," she said.

The audio in Shelley's helmet enhanced her voice so that he heard her even over the roar of burning munitions. He rolled and fired. The figure in the truck went over backward, hitting the dusty ground with an ugly bounce.

Karin scanned the squad map. "No indication of surviving enemy, but shrapnel from those rockets—"

"*Fall back!*" Shelley ordered on gen-com. Powered by his exoskeleton, he sprang to his feet and took off. "*Fall back! All speed!*"

Karin watched until he put a hundred meters behind him; then she switched to Holder, confirmed his ambush had gone off as planned; switched to Deng who was driving an ATV, racing to cut off her own insurgent incursion; switched to Valdez, who had finally joined up with another squad to quell a street battle in an ancient desert city.

"*Delphi, you there?*" Shelley asked.

"I'm here." Her voice hoarse, worn by use.

Dawn had come. All along the northern border the surviving enemy were in retreat, stopping their exodus only when hunting gunships passed nearby. Then they would huddle out of sight beneath camouflage blankets until the threat moved on. The incursion had gained no territory, but the insurgents had won all the same by instilling fear among the villages and the towns.

Karin had already seen Valdez and Holder and Deng back to their shelters. Now Shelley's squad was finally returning to their little fort.

"*Is Hawkeye done?*" he asked her.

She sighed, too tired to really think about it. "I don't know. Maybe."

"*I never liked him much.*"

Karin didn't answer. It wasn't appropriate to discuss another handler.

"*You still there?*"

"I'm here."

"*You want to tell me if this was a one-night-stand? Or are you going to be back tonight?*"

Exhaustion clawed at her and she wanted to tell him *no*. No, I will not be back. There wasn't enough money in the world to make this a good way to spend her life.

Then she wondered: when had it ceased to be about the money?

The war was five thousand miles away, but it was inside her head too; it was inside her dreams and her nightmares.

"*Delphi?*"

"I'm here."

In her worst nightmares, she lost voice contact. That's when she could see the enemy waiting in ambush, when she knew his position, his weaponry, his range . . . when she knew her clients were in trouble, but she couldn't warn them.

"You want me to put in a formal request for your services?" Shelley pressed. *"I can do that, if you need me to."*

It wasn't money that kept Karin at her control station. As the nightmare of the war played on before her eyes, it was knowing that the advice and the warnings that she spoke could save her soldiers' lives.

"It's best if you make a formal request," Karin agreed. "But don't worry—I'll be here."

—⁓—

Nightside on Callisto

A FAINT, STEADY vibration carried through the igloo's massive ice walls—a vibration that shouldn't have been there. Jayne heard it in her sleep. Age had not dulled her soldier's reflexes, honed by decades spent on watch against incursions of the Red. Her eyes snapped open. She held her breath. The vibration hummed in the walls, in the bed frame, in the mattress, perceivable even over Carly's raspy breathing.

Jayne reminded herself that the Red was far, far away, its existence bound to Earth, where it bled through every aspect of life—a relentless tide of information and influence shepherding the thoughts and actions of billions along paths determined by its unknowable goals. Whether the Red was alive, or aware, Jayne couldn't say, and she had no opinion either on its virtue. She only wanted to keep it out of the Shell Cities. Most of her life had gone to the long defense of their growing union, an association of scattered orbital habitats determined to stay free of the Red. But in retirement, Jayne had found new opportunities.

Less than twenty-four hours ago, her team of four had touched down on Callisto, Jupiter's outermost Galilean moon and the only one that lay beyond the gas giant's killing radiation belts. A raft of construction equipment had preceded them, including a gang of ten small mechs that had assembled a sprawling igloo in time for them to move in. It was the team's task to establish a prototype ice-mining station to supply the expansion of the Shell Cities.

Maybe the vibration was generated by some new construction activity at the launch rail? Probably that was it. But "probably" never was a sufficient explanation. Jayne slipped out from under the shared blanket, careful not to wake Carly, who'd crawled into bed just an hour ago. Each team member worked a staggered, twelve-hour shift. Jayne had taken the first rotation, and her night was almost through.

The air-skin membrane lining the walls and the ceiling sensed her movement and responded with a glimmer of vague gray illumination. Jayne stood up slowly on sleep-stiffened limbs. A century of existence had left her thin and tough and inclined to feel cold, so over a foundation of thermal underwear she added insulated slacks, a pullover of the same material, thin gloves for her hands, and cozy house boots for her feet—one more layer in the cocoon that protected them from the cold and vacuum beyond the igloos walls.

Jayne knew with utter certainty that they were alone in Jupiter system. The Red could not be here—the light speed lag in information flow kept it confined near Earth—and no other expedition had ventured so far in years. So their team was on its own, with no back up if something went wrong—which was why the four of them had been awarded this project: they were each experienced, competent, and expendable.

The bed chamber was sealed off from the rest of the igloo by an air-skin lock. Jayne touched the membrane. It felt smooth and hard beneath her gloved hand, but when she swept her fingers across it, the skin lock responded, pulling aside in neat, glassy ripples.

Massive blocks of ancient ice made up the igloo's walls and ceiling, insulating the interior spaces from background radiation, but it was the air skin that made the igloo habitable. A semi-intelligent, quasi-living tissue, the skin lined every chamber, locking in pressure, and providing heat and fresh air. If perforated it would self-seal, and its motility allowed it to repair even major tears.

Jayne stepped past the plastic-panel door into a central alcove with toilets and shower on either side. Two steps ahead, a lock on the right stood open to the easy room with its cushy inflatable furnishings, food stores, and oven, while on the left, another open lock hooked up to HQ, where the work was done. Jayne heard Berit speaking. She couldn't make out the words, but Berit's sharp, angry tone confirmed Jayne's first suspicion: something had gone wrong.

Jayne resisted the impulse to sprint into HQ. Age and experience had taught her to always attend to basics, so she slipped into the toilet first, and only when that necessity was out of the way did she trot around the corner.

Berit heard her coming and greeted her with a scowl. She was ninety-nine, an age that could be seen in the translucence of her brown skin, in the drape of tissue around her stern eyes, and in the thinning of her bright white hair. Like Jayne, Berit had lived most of her life as a soldier in the defense force and like Jayne, she'd been lucky, surviving to tell the tale. The two women had partnered on more assignments than either cared to remember. "What woke you up?" Berit snapped.

"The smell of trouble. Why am I hearing tones of displeasure in your voice?"

"Because I am not pleased."

Lorelei was their civilian engineer, a petite, soft-spoken woman who, at a hundred-and-three, was older even than Jayne. She provided more details without turning away from a 3-D model of the station. "Our mechs are tainted. Something's gotten into them and they aren't accepting commands."

"The Red followed us here," Berit added, with fatalistic certainty.

When Jayne joined them, they made a circle around the model. "How?"

Lorelei looked up, her deep blue eyes nestled in the folds and rough texture of her dark skin. Her hair was brilliant white and still thick despite the years, confined in a heavy braid at her shoulder. She opened her mouth to speak—and a high-pitched whistle screamed through the igloo. Jayne's ears popped. The air-skin lock rustled shut, sealing HQ from the rest of the station and muting the whistle, but Jayne could still hear a distant wail of escaping air.

"Pressure suits!" she barked. "Now! Go!"

The suits hung ready on the wall beside the external lock. Jayne had taken only two steps toward them when a faint *pop!* put an end to the whistle. The igloo shuddered as massive ice blocks groaned against each other. *Goddamnit*, Jayne thought, grabbing two suits and tossing them to Berit and Lorelei. *Goddamnit, if the roof comes down* . . .

They'd celebrated when they'd won this mission, knowing they'd gotten it because it *was* risky and because they were old. Medical technologists in the Shell Cities had learned to minimize the deterioration of old age so that hale and healthy lifespans stretched past a century, but inevitable, catastrophic failure still loomed: a blood vessel bursting in the brain, a heart chamber undergoing sudden collapse, a lung growing irreparably brittle. The cold fact was, none of them had much time left. If they didn't survive this mission, well, only a handful of unlived years would be lost. But in the meantime they were privileged to set foot on one of Jupiter's moons and to have the chance of leaving the Shell Cities just a little more secure.

And the goddamned roof was *not* going to come down. Not if Jayne could help it.

She grabbed a third pressure suit and stepped into it, pulling the edges together to let it seal.

A pressure suit was just another form of air skin, made to wrap around the body. An inch thick in most places, it was powered by slender, flexible fuel cells embedded across the back. Robotic carbon-fiber hands at the sleeve ends exactly mimicked every twitch of Jayne's own fingers, which remained safe and warm within the sleeves.

Using an artificial hand, Jayne reached up and grabbed her hood, preventing it from sealing. Lorelei and Berit were still wrapping their suits on. "Lorelei, stay here and get those mechs in order. Berit, get outside and figure out what the hell just happened. I'm going after Carly."

She released her hood, not waiting for an answer. It rolled across her face, where it sealed, shaped, and hardened.

The air-skin lock to the central alcove had sealed, but the color-coded indicator glowed green, confirming full pressure beyond. Jayne passed through, carrying Carly's suit with her. The lock sealed again behind her.

A glance around the alcove confirmed all the locks had closed. Those to HQ, the easy room, and the toilets, showed green, but the indicator beside the bedchamber flashed in calamitous red.

Jayne bit down on the inside of her lip, remembering Carly's warmth and her good humor. "Berit?"

"I'm heading out now," she answered over the suit radio. Then, "*Oh.*" A single word, the pain in it as sharp as shattered ice. "I see what you're looking at."

"I'm going in." Jayne brushed her fingers across the skin lock. Her suit stiffened as air was evacuated from the alcove, and for a moment she couldn't move. Then the suit's crosslinked cells adapted to the pressure change, and once again sensors picked up the motion of her body and echoed it, moving as she moved, tripling her strength—though if the power unit ever ran down, the pressure suit would become her diamond coffin.

She still held onto Carly's suit, for all the good it would do.

The air skin opened. Light that didn't belong illuminated the bedchamber with a faint glow. Their station was sited away from Jupiter and the Sun was too far away to make a difference, but a small measure of starlight spilled in through a ragged hole, three-feet wide and slanting up through a massive block of ice. The light wasn't enough to make out any details until the suit's faceplate switched to nightvision. Then Berit's voice sighed over the com. "Oh, *Carly*. Blood-red piss! She was trying to get to the lock!"

Carly's body lay face down against the floor, her legs and hips crushed beneath the ice that had fallen from the ceiling. Her fate had been set the moment Jayne decided to leave her sleeping— while Jayne's own bitter luck still held.

She forced herself to look away from the body, to look up. The air skin had been ripped open around the deep, ragged hole in the ice roof. Its tattered edges writhed, questing blindly for each other. More and more of it peeled away from the low ceiling, from the walls. It would keep peeling, until the torn edges could reach each other, and then it would seal. All this, Jayne took in at a glance—and then she noticed movement, just outside the hole: a mech, outlined against the stars.

All ten of the station mechs were the same model. They had a core carapace in the shape of a disk and roughly the size of a seat cushion, mounted on three highly flexible, telescoping legs. Each hemisphere of the carapace had a working arm. The upper half could swivel, so that the two arms could be positioned at any angle to one another. Most often, though, the arms were combined into a single limb for additional strength. By default, mechs stood with their legs at full extension, making them roughly waist high. Half-inch circles of cold blue light dotted their legs and made a glowing belt around their carapaces.

The mech on the igloo's roof had a subordinate drill unit set up at the edge of the hole. The drill was just a tool with no onboard intelligence. Its cylindrical column waited motionless, while the mech paced around it in what looked like frantic indecision. Jayne felt her skin crawl, watching it. Mechs should not behave that way. She wondered what directive had brought it to the igloo's roof.

"Lorelei?"

"Here." Lorelei's voice was a choked whisper.

"Tell me that mech showed up to repair the damage."

"I don't know why it's there. I can't know. Its directives have been changed. I can't get any data out of it. I can't get any instructions in. The mechs are talking to each other, but they won't communicate with me."

Mechs possessed a limited machine intelligence. Though they could learn by experience, they weren't remotely self-aware, and still . . . the directives that guided them could result in behavior that imitated volition in a truly unsettling way.

As Jayne watched, one of the mech's arms darted under its belly, then flashed out again, dropping a finger-sized cylinder through the hole. The cylinder fell in slow motion, bouncing off the mound of fallen ice before tumbling to the floor. A bang rod, Jayne realized—a small explosive used by the mechs to quarry the granite-hard ice at Callisto's surface.

"Get down!" Berit screamed over the suit's com system. Jayne was already moving, diving behind the bed just before the bang rod exploded with a brilliant flash. The floor jumped, a flash of heat washed past, and then Jayne rolled, the suit providing a smooth muscle-assist to get her to her feet again.

Ice flakes and frozen flecks of blood dropped like snow, blanketing a shallow crater, and the raw, red, frozen mass that had been Carly's body.

"Lorelei," Jayne asked in a steely voice, "did that mech just try to blow me up?"

Lorelei's mind was on other things. She spoke in breathy excitement. "I just found a record of a transmission from the landing pod, right before everything fell apart—"

"What are you talking about? The landing pod's sitting empty outside our front door. It's powered down."

"Power's back on," Lorelei said, her voice breaking. "There's some device in it we didn't know about. We're at war, Jayne—"

"I goddamn well know that!"

"—and we've just been hit! Whatever was in the pod pumped tainted directives into the mechs and changed their access codes. God knows what they're programmed to do now—"

"They're programmed to sabotage this mission," Berit growled over the com. "Because the Red doesn't want us growing. We should have seen this coming."

Jayne watched the mech reach out with a mechanical hand, disconnecting the tether that tied it to the drill subordinate. A second mech appeared, and immediately hopped down through the hole, dropping into the bedchamber with dreamlike lethargy. It was still falling when a six-inch jet of tightly focused blue flame spat from a torch gripped in its mechanical arm. Jayne fell back as it landed in the blast crater. Its telescoping legs flexed to absorb the impact, and then flexed again as it launched itself at her.

Screams filled the com, but Jayne ducked nimbly aside. The mech's carapace spun around as it landed, its arm extended as it tried to rake her with the torch. But it had been built for construction, not battle. Jayne was faster.

Dodging the flame, she threw herself on top of it, landing chest-first on its carapace. To her surprise, its legs collapsed under her weight. She rode it to the floor, using the suit's mechanical hands to hold onto its arm, forcing the fiery torch away from her face. With the suit's muscle-assist, she had as much strength as the mech, and to her astonishment, it stopped struggling after just a few seconds. Its torch switched off.

"What just happened?" Jayne whispered.

Lorelei answered over the com. "It summoned a crane to get the weight off its back. Logical response to baseline directive: 'don't damage yourself.' Now shut it down."

"How?"

"There's a panel on the carapace. Don't shift your weight. Just feel for it."

Jayne scowled. She was holding the mech's arm with both her mechanical hands, but now, cautiously, she let one go. As her carbon-fiber fingers slid around the carapace, the suit replicated the texture for her organic fingers. She found the panel, popped the release, slipped her hand inside.

"This is a whole keypad! What am I supposed to do?"

"Lower two corners. Top center. Press them all at once. Hold them down."

Jayne did it, suddenly aware of a faint vibration within the mech, only because it ceased.

"That's it," Lorelei said grimly. "One down. Nine to go."

But the mech didn't look like it had been shut down. The lights on its legs and carapace still glowed. "Lorelei, why are the lights still on?"

"They're self-powered. Ever tried finding a quiescent mech in the dark?"

Jayne snorted. "So that's it? That's all there is to it? We just switch them off? This is going to be—"

"Lorelei!" Berit's voice cut across the com, edged in panic. "Get outside now! Mechs are above you, drilling on the roof. Jayne—"

"On my way."

First, though, Jayne took the torch from the switched-off mech and used it to cut a five-foot length out of the twisted remains of the plastic bed frame. Steel would have been better, but at least now she had a weapon with better reach than the torch.

The torn air skin had continued to peel off the wall, rolling down so far that it was writhing around her, its raw edges beginning to seal. Jayne took a giant step to get on top of it. Then she lobbed her plastic rod through the hole in the roof, vaulting after it with a powerful muscle-assist from the suit.

Under Callisto's low gravity, she shot up through the hole. Her mechanical fingers hooked over the rim of ice and she hauled herself out onto the roof.

The igloo's ice blocks had been quarried from beneath the dusty regolith. Impurities in the ice infused it with a gray, piebald cast that gleamed only faintly under the star-spangled sky. The land around was even darker: a gray, granular plane that rolled away to low, encircling hills with steep profiles that rose in black outline against the stars. Frost glimmered faintly, looking like a mist laid across the rounded peaks.

The construction site was a half mile away, on flat ground, where steel bars for the launch rail were piled up into their own small hill. The mechs should have been at work on the rail bed, but Jayne saw nothing moving out there. Closer in, the landing pod crouched on bent legs, sparkling like gold foil. Jayne spotted two mechs loitering near it. Then she turned, to look across the flat roof.

The blast hole was close to one end. In the open area beyond it Berit chased a retreating mech. Another circled around to where three drill units bored into the ice above HQ, each one sending up a plume of frost that glittered in the starlight. Jayne imagined the mechs' simple logic: drills bore holes into ice; bang rods drop into holes; heavy, ice-insulated roofs get blown asunder.

The third mech on the roof was the one that had dropped the bang rod. It skittered toward her around the edge of the blast hole, but it didn't have a torch and it had already used its explosive. Jayne didn't see how it could be dangerous, so she circled the hole to meet it.

It saw her move, and hesitated.

Jayne didn't. Taking two long strides, she threw herself at it, just as she had with the other—but this mech anticipated her. Its legs flexed and it jumped out of reach. Jayne slammed against the roof, sliding several feet past the hole, only remembering to dig in with her mechanical fingers a moment before she went hurtling over the roof's edge.

Over the com, Berit's breath came fast and heavy. "Guess what, Jaynie? The mechs have figured out that move. I can't get near them."

Jayne groaned—"Thanks for letting me know"—and got back onto her feet.

The mech stood, unmoving, a few meters away. "It looks confused," Jayne muttered. Maybe it didn't know what to do next; maybe its directives didn't include all the necessary details of murder when the first assault had failed.

Unlike the mech, Jayne could come up with alternatives.

An image of the blood-red pulp of Carly's body flashed across her mind. Returning to the hole, she grabbed the abandoned drill unit. The tool probably massed as much as she did, but this was low-grav Callisto and Jayne was wearing a powered suit. It was no problem at all to hurl the drill straight at the mech's carapace.

The mech ducked by collapsing its telescoping legs. It dropped with astonishing speed and the drill shot harmlessly past it, spinning away in a trajectory that took it beyond the roof and far out over the gray flats. So. Projectiles weren't going to work. Jayne bent to retrieve her plastic staff, determined to give that a try. As she straightened up again, the two mechs from below vaulted onto the roof above HQ.

One at a time, Jaynie, she reminded herself, and with an overhead stroke she brought the rod down hard against the first mech's carapace. The staff snapped in two. The mech took no damage at all. Jayne flung away the remnant in disgust. So much for that idea—and now they had to contend with four mechs on the roof instead of just two.

The drills were unattended, but they continued to work, boring ever deeper into the igloo. Jayne turned her attention to them. There was no way she was going to let another chamber get blown. She bounded past the blast hole, toward the nearest drill. Ice flakes showered her as she reached it.

The drill stood thigh high, a slender cylinder hot enough to turn the falling flakes to vapor. Jayne grabbed it with her mechanical hand and yanked—but bolts locked it to the ice. She crouched, searching the drill for a panel like the one on the mech, but she couldn't find one.

"Lorelei, you still alive?"

"So far."

"How do I shut off a drill?"

"You don't unless you know how to send drill codes."

"Fine, then. Berit? Watch my back." Flicking on the torch she'd taken from the mech, Jayne started cutting. The drill shook when she sliced away the first bolt holding it to the ice. It bucked when she cut the second. And then it shut down. Safety override?

Two other drills were running. With Berit standing guard, she cut bolts on both of them, and when they unbalanced, they shut down too.

"Nice," Berit said. "But we still have nine hostile mechs to contend with." She was standing a few feet away, jumping at any mech that dared to come close.

"Lorelei," Jayne asked, "where are you?"

"In the landing pod."

Jayne glanced at the gold-foil dome resting on the regolith below. The door was closed. "Okay, stay there. Berit, let's get out to the construction site, pick up some explosives and maybe a rebar or two to smash these Red traitors."

"Jayne, no!" Lorelei snapped. "Do *not* damage the mechs!"

"Oh," Berit said. "I guess you didn't see her hurl that drill unit."

"What?" Lorelei sounded outraged. "Jayne, we need the mechs. Every one of them, or this project fails."

"We've already lost the mechs," Jayne shot back. She longed to get her mechanical hands around a steel rebar and test that against a carapace, maybe find out what a mech was made of inside. "Carly is dead and this project *has* failed."

"Carly is dead," Lorelei agreed, speaking softly now, hurriedly. "But we're still here and the Shell Cities are still going to need every crystal of water we can send them and we're not going to be able to send even one drop without mechs to build the launch rail. I am *not* lifting off from here until that rail is built."

"Goddamn it, Lorelei. You're the expert on the mechs, and you said you can't communicate with them, you can't override their rogue programming—"

"I can't! Not until they're shut down. *Manually* shut down, each and every one of them, just like that mech in the bedchamber." Her voice softened again. "Then they can be reset to factory specs. They won't know how to build anymore, but we can teach them that."

Jayne turned to Berit. Her faceplate was black in the dim light, but her bitter mood came through in her voice. "You hear that, Jaynie? The first rule of this little battle is 'do no harm.' You better give me that torch before the rule slips your mind."

Lorelei wanted to close off the honey hole.

The mechs had a hybrid, bio-mechanical architecture that required them to resupply and re-power every twelve hours or so inside the honey hole—an excavated ice cave out by the construction site, stocked with fuel cells and organic supplies.

Jayne, though, wasn't willing to leave four functioning mechs on the roof. Three of them probably still had bang rods. Why didn't they use them? Maybe they didn't know how. Without a drill hole to stuff them into or a blast hole to toss them down, their simple behavioral algorithms might be stymied.

They could learn, though. They'd watched Jayne take down a mech and now they retreated if Jayne or Berit approached them. But if the women turned their backs, the mechs approached, carrying torches and saws in their mechanical hands like a pod of metallic zombies.

"Hey," Jayne said. "I'm going to walk away. If one starts to follow, you fall in behind. Push it close to me."

Berit nodded. "Go."

Jayne set off at a slow pace across the roof.

Berit hissed. "All four are behind you."

Jayne didn't turn to look. Instead, she picked up the feed from Berit's helmet and watched the mechs coming after her at a disturbingly fast pace. They were eight meters away, seven, six—one walked in front, two followed, and the fourth came behind. Berit trailed them, several steps back.

"I'll take the one closest to me," Jayne said.

"I'll get the laggard."

"Three, two, one, *now*."

Jayne turned and jumped. The mech she'd targeted jumped too, but not fast enough. They hit in midair. She spilled over its back, but managed a clawed grip on its carapace, hauling it down with her. It had a torch. She scrambled on top of it, holding its arm down with her foot. Flame touched ice, vapor roiled up, turning almost instantly into snow, while beneath her weight the mech went still. Jayne popped open its panel and slammed mechanical fingers down on the three keys, but she was breathing too hard to feel the mech's faint vibrations; she couldn't tell if the vibrations had stopped. "Did it shut down?" she panted. "Did it?"

"Move!" Berit shouted.

Jayne saw the bright blue light of another torch darting toward her face. She rolled. A line of heat seared her forearm, followed by a blade of cold. A muscle-assist popped her back onto her feet as two torches jabbed toward her. She jumped back, pursued by a pair of mechs, each with a torch in one hand, a saw in the other. Pain like a vice gripped her forearm.

She glanced at the wound. The torch had cut a line in her suit, but it had not cut quite through. She pinched the burnt edges together, helping the suit's healthy tissue to meet and seal. Then she jumped again to avoid the oncoming mechs. With chagrin, she realized they'd learned to work together in their attack—doubtless from the very recent example of cooperative assault that she and Berit had shown them.

"Okay, Jaynie?" Berit asked.

"So far."

They'd brought down one mech each, but there were still two more on the roof. Both pursued Jayne, torches out in a coordinated rush—until Berit tackled one from behind. It went down. Berit slapped open the panel, decommissioned it, and was up again in seconds, while Jayne led the last one on a merry chase.

A column of snow marked every dropped torch. Jayne wove between them to distract the mech, while Berit stood still, trying to go unnoticed in the mech's busy visual field. Jayne slipped past her, the mech followed, and Berit pounced. Her breathing came ragged over the com. "That's five down, five to go."

Jayne made a quick circuit of the roof, gathering up the torches and switching them off before they could melt all the way down to the membrane. "*Now* we take care of the honey hole."

Berit was still pulling hard for air. "I hope you're planning to help out a little more this time."

Jayne snorted. "I thought it was very noble of me, to be the bait."

They jumped down from the roof. Lorelei came out of the gold-foil dome of the pod. She held up a rectangular wafer for them to see. It was no more than one by two inches, thin as foil. "Light a torch," she said.

Jayne complied. The blue flame was a needle in the dark. "That's it, then? That's the source of the rogue code? And it's the only one?"

"It's the only one I could find." Lorelei laid the wafer down on the ice and stepped back. "Burn it."

Jayne did. Then she ground it with her boot and burned the remnants again.

As they crossed the dusty regolith to the construction site, Jayne spotted a flock of tiny lights a few hundred yards away. "The mechs," she announced. If not for the glowing circles dotting their legs and carapaces, they might have come unseen. "They must have been recharging in the honey hole."

"No," Berit said grimly. "I think they were taking notes."

Lorelei stopped. "I don't understand. Why are they hauling rebars?"

The mechs' legs flashed as they stepped swiftly through the dust and after a few seconds Jayne saw what Berit and Lorelei had spotted first: three of the mechs were armed with long steel rebars from the construction site.

"Dammit, Jayne!" Berit groused. "They saw you hit that mech with a rod."

Lorelei turned. Jayne couldn't see her face, but her voice sounded scandalized. "You hit a mech? I told you—"

"This was before you told me."

"Did you damage it?"

Jayne snorted. "Sadly, no. I used a plastic rod. The mechs have improved my example. They've got steel."

"We aren't going to be able to get close to them," Berit warned.

By this time, the mechs were hardly a hundred yards away, and moving fast.

"We could just walk out on the ice," Lorelei said in a small voice. "Lead them away until they run out of power."

"If they've just come out of the honey hole they've got twelve hours. Our suits won't last that long, and besides, I don't want to give them a chance to blow the rest of the igloo."

"Then what do we do?"

Jayne touched the seam that marked the healed tear in the forearm of her suit. A pressure suit was just another form of air skin. Without power, both turned into diamond-hard crystal. "We need to incapacitate the mechs without harming them."

"Right," Berit said with sharp impatience. "And how do we do that?"

"Let's go back to the igloo. I have an idea."

Jayne took everyone up to the roof. With a muscle-assist from the suits, the jump was easy.

"There are two ways we can lose this battle," Jayne reminded. "We lose if the mechs kill us and we lose if we kill the mechs—but if it comes down to it and we're going to lose anyway, let's lose the second way. Agreed?"

"We're going to win," Lorelei said in a hollow voice. Berit echoed the sentiment.

Jayne shrugged. "Fine, then. Let's win."

She jumped down through the blast hole into the blown bed-chamber.

During the time Jayne had been outside, the ragged edges of the room's air skin had knit together, joining just a few feet above the floor. With the seal complete, the flexible membrane had hardened into a smooth, curved surface. Jayne kept her feet when she landed on it, but she couldn't stop herself from sliding until she fetched up against the exposed wall of ice.

It occurred to Jayne that not an hour before, she'd been sleeping in this room, in the cocoon of Carly's warmth.

"No time for sightseeing," Berit chided gently.

"Hush, child. Don't annoy your elders."

Jayne fired up her torch. Braced against the wall, she bent low and started cutting.

At the first touch of the flame, the air skin caved in, dropping away from the heat. Jayne bent lower and kept cutting, until slowly, slowly, the flame sliced the air skin open. The small space enclosed by the air skin had already started to re-pressurize, so for a second ice flakes geysered through the crack. Then, along the cut edges, the air skin softened, again becoming a flexible, rippling fabric as it strove to seal up the cut.

Jayne didn't let that happen. She jammed her foot through the crack and kicked it wider. Lorelei jumped down to help, folding the air skin back while Jayne kept cutting, separating a large sheet of it and exposing again the remains of the room.

Berit stayed on the roof, watching the approaching mechs and counting down the time to their arrival. "You've got maybe twenty seconds. Okay, ten. That's it! The first one just jumped to the roof."

Jayne passed the torch to Lorelei. "Be ready to make the last cut, but only when I tell you, not before."

It was too dark to see her face past the helmet, but she took the torch with steady hands.

With a corner of the membrane gripped in one mechanical hand, Jayne jumped back up through the blast hole. All five remaining mechs were already on the roof. Berit stood facing them, with the hole at her back.

The air skin writhed in Jayne's grip, rolling up and down her arm. She hadn't been afraid of the mechs before—not really, truly afraid. She'd known they were dangerous. After the first bang rod, she'd known her life and Berit's and Lorelei's could end as quickly as Carly's had, but the mech assault had happened so fast she'd had no time to really be afraid . . . until now.

Of the five mechs, three held ten-foot-long steel rebars, while two used their dexterous double arms to hold torches and drills. Jayne had a nasty suspicion the drills weren't meant for drilling.

"Look out!" she shouted, as a mech hurled its drill dead-on at Berit.

Berit dropped flat. The drill spun past her, disappearing into the dark as the mechs swarmed.

"Get up!" Jayne growled as the mechs came after Berit—a pack of mechanical zombies armed with sticks and stones and fire. "Berit, *move*."

"Stop worrying about me and do your job!" Berit snapped, still lying face down.

"Fine, then!" Jayne tugged hard on the air skin. "Lorelei—cut it and jump!"

Berit waited another second, until the mechs were in rebar range, then she vaulted backward, landing on her feet. The startled mechs slowed. Berit turned and ran. The zombie mob took off after her, while Lorelei shouted, "Jumping!"

As Berit darted past the blast hole, Lorelei appeared at its mouth. She hauled herself out, clutching another corner of the air skin in one mechanical hand. They now had a sheet of it, cut free from the room. Severed from its power source, the skin had only seconds before it froze into a crystal coffin. Already Jayne felt it getting stiff in her hands. She got ready, knowing they'd have only one chance to make this work.

Alongside the blast hole there was only a narrow strip of intact roof. The mechs bunched together as they passed around it, just as Jayne had hoped.

"Stand firm," she said. "I'm going . . . *now!*"

With the air skin gripped in both hands, she stepped away from the mechanical mob. Lorelei held the other end and the skin became a trembling gray curtain between them. Lorelei stood behind it, but Jayne kept in sight. The mechs saw her and pursued, sweeping past Lorelei. As soon as they'd gone by, Lorelei cut behind them, bending the air skin to form a U.

Now came the critical part. Could they close the circle? Jayne waited an extra second. Then she turned and darted back along the roof's edge. The air skin billowed around the mechs as they turned to cut her off. And then she was past them. Lorelei was only a step away.

"Pull it tight!" Jayne warned.

An eight-foot rebar came spinning out of the mech mob. Jayne felt betrayed—she'd never taught them to throw a rebar! She ducked, but not fast enough. Steel slammed against her shoulder, knocking her down and sending her skidding across the ice—but she didn't let go of the air skin. Her mechanical hands kept their grip, even as she plunged over the roof's edge.

Jayne stirred, wondering how she'd come to be in the easy room. She was stretched out on a couch, a blanket pulled up to her chin. Berit sat in a cushy chair a few feet away, watching her with a critical expression. Jayne tried to speak, but she had to swallow a few times before she had enough moisture in her throat to ask, "What the hell is going on?"

Berit leaned back in her chair. Her eyes narrowed. "You fell off the roof. If you remember, that wasn't in the plan."

It all started coming back. "Where's Lorelei?"

"I'm here, Jayne!" Her gentle voice came sailing out of HQ.

"As it turns out," Berit went on, "falling off the roof probably saved us all. The air skin wasn't going to pull tight enough around the mechs to confine them—not until you went over. Then Lorelei jumped after you and dragged the mechs down with her. By the time they knew what hit them, the air skin had crystallized around them and they couldn't move. All but one. It got out, but I tackled it and shut it down."

"And the rest?"

"We cut them out one at a time and turned them off. Then we reset them all to factory specs. Lorelei's loading some basic construction directives into them now."

"So we got lucky again?"

"We got lucky. The Red didn't beat us this time. You did good, Jaynie. I'm proud of you. You didn't harm even a single enemy."

Jayne snorted. "Let's both try to live a few years longer—and make up for it next time."

—∿∿—

Attitude

Our Only Export is Entertainment

The announcer's voice boomed across the arena as I plummeted feet first toward the alpha fin of the central pylon. I caught my name—Juliet Alo—but nothing else because I was playing Attitude, and in the climactic seconds of the championship round, all my brain power was consumed with calculating trajectories across the three dimensions of zero-gee.

I was only a rookie, but I could extrapolate a player's destination a moment after launch. Sometimes I knew where players would go before they did—and that gave me time to evade them.

I reached the alpha fin and kicked off again with the ball of my foot, extending into a needle posture to shoot across the zero-gee arena with my arms pressed to my sides, legs straight, toes pointed in an aerodynamic configuration aided by the smooth lines of my gold bodysuit. An opposing player in the dark-purple suit of Team August streaked in to intercept my trajectory—too late. Frustration lined a face framed by the gel-padded bars of his helmet as I whispered past his outstretched fingertips on my way to a calculated rendezvous with the ball.

The arena we played in was a vast oval, sixty meters in length and caged by softly glowing red filaments that flared a penalty if touched by a player or by the ball. Up and down had no real meaning, but we oriented anyway with a gradient from deep-water blue at the base to brilliant white at the summit. The central pylon was an irregular corkscrew studded with fins small and large and set at random angles in an array that changed every quarter, never twice the same. Goal rings were hung at the base and the summit.

The number of spectators present in the zero-gee hub of Stage One was small—just the players from other teams, the Stage One staff, and, for every game, at least four "special guests"—Attitude fans flown to LEO at the A-League's expense, because "Attitude is for everyone."

It was a slogan, but the A-League took it seriously. Fans around the world could watch sponsored showings at home or they could spend a little to purchase admission to live, 3-D renderings of the game in theaters, sharing the experience with hundreds of others, at a ticket price that shifted with a region's median income. And of course there was gear, and gambling, and commercial endorsements, but there were also prizes and scholarships and a network of authorized trainers around the world sponsoring camps and competitions for future players. Though only in its fifth year of existence, Attitude had become one of the most popular spectator sports in or off the world.

I played for Team November. We'd won three of five games in the final series against Team August, and with time running out in Game 6, one more score would give us the championship.

I pulled in my knees, executed a flip, and hammered my feet against the jelly membrane of a static drum, arresting my momentum just as the spindle-shaped A-ball slammed into my hands.

Min Tao had thrown it hard, with so much spin it almost tore out of my grip. Fierce screams rose up from the arena audience and after a delay of a fractional second—the time required for the crowd noise generated by the nearest theaters to reach us—there were groans and gasps and then a deafening cheer as I secured my grip on the ball.

Team August players in their dark uniforms raced to set up a defense as I cocked my arm and passed for the goal—

Fake passed.

I pumped my arm but held onto the ball, drawing out an opposing player who'd been lurking for a chance to intercept. He dove toward me, blocking my line to the goal ring—but I never meant to go straight in anyway. I counted silently, the same count Min Tao was keeping as he clung to a nearby fin, gleaming in Team November's gold uniform—and at zero we both launched.

Our trajectories met in wide-open air. The screams of the crowd reverberated around us as I flat-handed off Min Tao's shoulder, shifting my trajectory toward the goal ring as my teammates converged from all sides to block Team August's players.

I scanned the moving field, assuring myself no one could block me before I shot through the goal ring and scored. The game was mine to win.

Then I saw Cherise Caron moving—a third year veteran and Team August's best player. She relayed with a teammate, picking up momentum from the exchange along with a trajectory shift. In my head I extrapolated her course. Cherise would hit a summit fin where she would have to align and launch again to block my goal. I'd studied every play she'd made over three seasons and knew she had the skill to do it, but she did not have the time.

The score was mine. The game, mine. The equation was set and nothing could change my flight so I relaxed, turning my head to watch her as she reached the fin.

Something happened then, that I could not explain. Her momentum reversed so quickly it was as if a digital record skipped in time. All my calculations were thrown off by at least three-tenths of a second as she darted to intercept me, and before I could twist to protect the ball it was gone from my hands. She passed the ball on the fly, hurling it to a teammate waiting halfway to blue. Our backfield was left playing catch-up as Team August relayed the ball past fins and static drums. Then they blocked our lone defender before a player took the ball through the goal ring for an easy score.

The crowd roared, half in outraged disbelief, half in astonished joy.

The coaches liked to remind us that the only thing Stage One exports to Earth is entertainment.

We did a raging business that game.

———

Integrity is Everything

I came up to Stage One nine months ago, debarking from the space plane as a wonder-struck recruit. After the first ten minutes I was so nauseous I lost my lunch, heaving into a specially designed barf bag—and that was the only time I ever questioned my decision to play for the Attitude League.

The coaches and the medical staff helped us with the transition, and then we were herded into the huge arena—all of the season's first-year players together, with the veterans beside us. I want to say it was dreamlike, but if so it was a disturbing dream in which I foundered, nearly helpless in zero gee, bumping into other lost and frightened rookies just like me, while breathing in chill air laden with the stink of vomit and sweat and plastic volatiles. I felt lost, vulnerable, nauseous—but triumphant too because I'd made it.

Against all odds I'd won a place in the A-League and a home in low Earth orbit as a probationary citizen of Stage One.

Zaid Hackett came to speak to us. Known around the world simply as "Zaid," she was CEO of Stage One and the architect of this house of dreams. A small woman, already seventy years old, with close-cropped curly silver hair, light-colored eyes, and striking dark, red-brown skin. That day she wore knit pants and a short pullover that didn't quite hide a paunch, and though she spoke to us in a soft, husky voice, everything she said had resonance, as if the pent-up energy inside her escaped as a low vibration in every word, spilling purpose into the world.

Who else could have established Stage One? Though we were still under construction, with a build-out that would take many more years, we were the first-ever city in space. Other habitats existed in low Earth orbit, but we were the only one to rotate, generating a half-gee of pseudogravity at the end of the spokes that circled the zero-gee core. Donations had financed the initial startup, but every stage since had been paid for with revenue generated by the A-League. Our fans financed the future, creating a permanent foothold in space for the people of Earth.

Zaid Hackett was a visionary, but she was a realist too who

reminded us of the hard truth: "Given the cost of access to space, only a few people will ever be privileged to go up. Those of us who are here carry with us the hopes and dreams of millions who will never have the chance to go forward into a wider future. Remember that. Remember them. Our fans will support us only so long as we are worthy of their support. In the Attitude League, integrity is everything."

My team, Team November, had lost Game 6 and I was furious. We left the victors celebrating in the arena and sculled in sullen silence through the short passage to our locker room—a small chamber curved to fit within the rim of the core. The twelve of us gathered there, floating with knees folded, our gold uniforms damp with sweat but still bright—a sharp contrast to our dark, disbelieving murmurs.

Coach Szarka came in last. He was a passionate, determined man and I'm sure he would have delivered a memorable speech about how we would return, stronger for our loss, to win both Game 7 and the season championship—except I didn't give him the chance. If I let my anger cool I would talk myself into doing nothing. So as the door closed I held fast to a wall loop and blurted what I knew to be the truth: "We were cheated out of a victory! Cherise could not have done what she did without over-enhancing. I wasn't the only one counting off the time. Everyone here knows I'm right."

Dead silence followed. Never before had there been an accusation of cheating in the A-League. My heart beat once, twice, three times as Coach stared at me, too stunned to speak. My face, already puffy in the absence of gravity, swelled a little more as I flushed, overtaken by an emotion somewhere between shame, terror, and outrage.

I turned to my teammates for support. Several looked frightened. Bruna Duarte, a first-year like me, looked confused. But Min Tao—who was both team captain and our top player—encouraged me with a nod, so I turned back to Coach and made my argument, pretending I didn't hear the quaver in my voice:

"We've all enhanced our response times. That's no secret. We operate at the maximum allowed by the League—which means we all know the exact time it should have taken Cherise to perform that V-launch. But she beat that time—and the only way she could have done that was by cheating. She over-enhanced."

Min Tao hooked a foot under a loop and straightened his lean, compact body. "Juliet's right. I counted too and Cherise could not have *legally* moved that fast."

It was as if he'd given the team permission to see the truth. Everyone started talking, insisting they'd suspected too. I raised my voice to be heard. "I want to file a protest."

Bruna scowled at me, but others agreed:

"Juliet's right."

"If we're going to file a protest, we need to do it now."

"I *knew* something was off."

Coach listened and nodded, looking grim. "It's our duty to report it. I'll take it to the league."

The Millions

We filed out, eager to get up the spoke to Stage One's rotating rim before Team August left the arena. With towels in hand to mop up our game sweat, we mobbed the portal. The transit pod carried only six passengers at a time, so I made sure I was at the front of the crush.

I was frightened by what I'd done. No one was going to be happy about it. Not even my teammates, not even if we were given the victory, because no one wanted to win the championship like that, post-game, on a technicality. Team August would hate me for it, and the league officials would be furious that I'd cast doubt on the integrity of the A-League. Would my career even survive?

The portal door slid open. I launched myself into the waiting pod right behind Bruna, following her to a backseat and buckling in. The transit pod was a rectangular brick with a transparent canopy. Blue Earth loomed overhead, but I only glanced at it before my gaze shifted to the oncoming gray wall that was Spoke-1. It swept toward us, huge and remorseless, one of only two complete spokes in our partially built city. Stage One would eventually grow into a spoked ring of habitable spaces, but we were still building the frame of the ring and so far our "city" occupied less than thirty degrees of arc at the end of Spoke-1, with an empty habitat as counterbalance at the end of Spoke-2. There was not room or resources to house a separate construction crew, so it was the players who did the work, putting in hours outside every day before practice.

The other four seats filled, the pod door slid shut, and behind it the portal closed.

"Why would she do it?" Bruna asked, loudly enough to include everyone.

Angelo answered her, a second-year player with an ego that outran his game skills. "So she can *win*. What do you think?"

"We all want to win," Min Tao said from his seat in the front row. "But we don't cheat. I've played against Cherise three seasons and she's never cheated before. Why now?"

"Money," Angelo said. "Why else?"

Money.

As players, we earned a respectable salary, but no one expected to get rich playing Attitude. Though the A-League took in vast sums of money, nearly all of it went into the maintenance and expansion of Stage One. As players, it was our privilege to be part of that. The league allowed us three seasons of play. At the end of that time, our names would go to the top of the list for subsidized family housing.

But bringing family up? We had to pay for that.

So money still mattered. Money always does.

As Spoke-1 reached us, we launched, the pod dropping onto the spoke's track in what felt like a sudden, sharp fall into gravity— or at least the pseudogravity generated by the centripetal force of the station's spin. We plummeted down the track, and a few seconds later an automated docking process synced us with the rim portal.

I was out of the transit pod as soon as the doors opened. The half-gee pull meant we walked, all of us hurrying because we had only a little time to shower and dress before the losers' post-game press conference—but as I neared my apartment I was distracted by a faint buzz, a sound I couldn't place.

"Hey!" Bruna said behind me. "Is that a fly? How did a fly get here?"

I ducked and backed against the wall as a silver insect buzzed above my head.

But it wasn't an insect. Though no bigger than a housefly, it was something mechanical, humming on iridescent wings that supported an oblong body, gray and hard to focus on.

"Crush it!" Min Tao shouted. He bounded past Bruna and jumped at the thing. It swerved, but Min Tao was faster. He flattened it against the ceiling, landing in a graceful crouch.

"Brutal," Bruna said. "Was that your lost toy?"

Min Tao held the lifeless thing in his palm for us to see. "Mech-skeeter. Someone smuggled a swarm of them up my first year."

The body of the device was an array of tiny, feathery plumes; from the sheen of its crushed wings, I suspected it was powered by light.

"So what's a mech-skeeter?" I asked.

"An assay device, to analyze air quality. Hypersensitive. Gambling operations use them to track the physical condition of athletes. Breathe on it"—he did—"and it'll ID you and measure your fitness by reading the chemicals in your breath." He looked up with a grin that made me wonder if he was joking. "Kill them," he advised as he opened the door to his room. "Or all your secrets are lost."

I stood beneath an endlessly recycling stream of hot water in the shower's tight confines, keeping my elbows close to my body as I washed my short hair. A scroll tacked to the shower wall showed the victors' post-game interview, with the twelve Team August players in their locker room, ready to answer questions from around the world. Most of the questions though went to their star player.

"Cherise, how do you explain your phenomenal performance?"

Cherise was a striking, sharp-featured woman of twenty-five, her skin smooth, and made milky by an absence of sunlight. "Three years of hard work," she said as I tapped the scroll to activate a facial analysis program. No alerts went up. She wasn't lying, but then the proper question hadn't been asked. "But also, the entire team is hungry to do what's never been done before, to win the Attitude championship two years in a row. We *can* do it. We *will* do it, now that we've made it to Game 7."

"Cherise, many of your fans wondered if Game 6 would be the last you ever played. Now you've earned one more, but this must be an emotional time for you, so close to the end of your career. Can you share your feelings with us?"

"It's tremendously sad. My time on Stage One has been the most meaningful of my life, and it will be hard to go home."

Her teammates gasped at her answer. I caught my breath, shutting off the water so I could hear better as the press corps fired off questions:

"Cherise, are you saying you're returning to Earth?"

"Are you saying you won't stay aboard Stage One?"

"Are you giving up citizenship?"

We were all shocked. Several players who'd finished their allotted three seasons had chosen to give up their claim to permanent housing and return to the world, but it was different with Cherise. She'd become the face of Attitude, widely considered the best who'd ever played. For her not to stay ... it was as if a queen should abdicate her throne.

I toweled off, taking the scroll with me as I stepped out of my tiny bathroom into my tiny apartment. The bed was a narrow platform accessed by a ladder, with storage underneath. A narrow desk was built into the opposite wall. There was nothing else, but it was enough.

I slapped the scroll against the wall, continuing to watch while I pulled on leggings and a team jersey. I was combing my black hair into neat lines when Team August signed off with a rousing cheer, *"August for the win!"*

I watched Cherise as she pumped her fist in the air along with the rest of the team, and I saw an imbalance in the gesture, as if her shoulders, elbows, and wrists were not quite synchronized. It was subtle, something I could see only because I'd studied her so closely for three years, but it was enough to convince me my protest had not been a mistake.

The league established a limit on neural enhancement because anything greater resulted in painful damage to joints and nerves that presented first as a loss of coordination. It horrified me to imagine Cherise crippled, and for what? To play just one more game? To win the championship bonus? And what was that worth? I knew the answer: one flight, one-way, on the space plane. That was all. Not enough to sacrifice your reputation and your health.

Bruna and Angelo were waiting for me in the corridor.

"Did you see the way she moved?" Bruna asked, her dark eyes and charcoal skin in contrast with close-cropped hair that she colored gold like our uniforms.

I nodded. "I can't believe she would do it, just for a chance at the bonus."

"It's not the bonus," Angelo said. He was petite and brown, with big hands, a sharp nose, and an annoying certainty about all his opinions, but I always listened to him anyway, because mostly he was right. "Half the world knows her name. If she retires with two championships in three years of play, the endorsement fees she'll command—"

"In the *millions*," I realized.

"That's right, baby girl," Angelo said. "Integrity is everything, right up until the day you leave Stage One."

Sportsmanship

Bruna, Angelo, and I were the last of the team to arrive in the press room. We walked into an ominous silence. Everyone else was already seated behind a long, elevated table, with Team November's hawk logo projected behind them. Facing the podium was a wall monitor used to stitch together the faces of media personalities from around the world to create an illusion of a collocated audience—except no one was there. The monitor was a neutral gray. Coach Szarka stood near it, his back turned to us, head bent in a whispered conference with Dob Irish, the League's marketing director. Both looked up as we came in.

"Take a seat," Coach said.

I went first, sitting next to Min Tao, who met my gaze with a grim expression.

Dob Irish took over. "The press conference is cancelled," he announced in a blunt, angry voice. He was a small but broad-shouldered man of florid complexion, outgoing, and well-known for his abundant smiles. I'd never seen him angry before—but cheating scandals were new to the A-League, and I approved of his outrage. "Marketing has been charged with containing the damage generated by today's sorry incident. The A-League prospers only so long as we maintain our reputation for fairness and respect for one another, but the poor sportsmanship displayed here today puts us all at risk."

Beside him, Coach Szarka's scowl became so deep his eyebrows met. "That is enough, Dob. You may not like it, but we had a legitimate reason for doubt. It was our *duty* to file a protest—"

"Tarnishing the reputation of our most beloved player because she snatched the championship away from you."

"Get out, Dob, before I do something we'll both regret."

Dob opened his mouth, reconsidered, and disappeared out the door.

I was so shocked, I could hardly breathe. I felt worse when Coach Szarka turned his scowl on us, because I knew what was coming.

"In response to our protest, Cherise's reaction time was tested by Dr. Kyre immediately following the locker-room interview. She passed that test. So August is the legitimate winner of Game 6. The A-League requests all players refrain from discussing the incident or responding to any questions about over-enhancement. Dismissed—all but you, Juliet. I want a word with you."

I felt cold and hot all at once, exposed and ruined and betrayed—because I knew what I'd seen. "They're covering it up," I whispered.

Min Tao put his hand on mine. "We'll talk later," he said as our teammates filed behind us, eager to escape.

I nodded, not even noticing when he disappeared. Quiet descended and I was alone behind the podium, staring at Coach Szarka. He said, "I'm not going to yell at you. I think we did the right thing. It's important we all police the integrity of the league—but this time we were wrong. Zaid has asked that you visit Cherise and offer your apology. I advise you to do it. A reputation for poor sportsmanship is not going to help you make it to your second season."

My hot flush was gone and all I felt was cold. "I was not the one who cheated."

"No one cheated," Coach insisted. "Apologize, Juliet, and hope we can put this behind us."

From the day I first heard of Stage One, I wanted to be part of it, this daring future aimed at building a city in space through the enthusiasm and the contributions of all the people of Earth . . . a city on the edge of the high frontier.

Skeptics had laughed at the business plan and called it a scam. Finance an orbital habitat from the revenue earned by a professional sports league? It could never happen!

But I was sixteen, not yet conquered by cynicism, and I thought, *Why not?* For decades professional sports had built mega-corporations, luxury stadiums, athletic complexes, and individual fortunes all around the world. What if all that money was channeled instead into Stage One?

I read the player qualifications, and knew they were within my reach. I'd gone from champion gymnastics in childhood to a national ranking in volleyball as a teen, so I had the necessary athleticism. Fluency in two languages was required. I was a native English speaker, knew Spanish, and had an acquaintance with Mandarin. My lack of height, which had limited my prospects in volleyball, was an advantage in the A-League, where the height restriction was 178 centimeters, because smaller people consume fewer resources and require less living space.

I applied three times before I was accepted. Afterward, I did a hundred interviews, bubbling with joy through every one of them, knowing I was one of the luckiest people in the world.

I did not apologize.

I returned to my apartment instead, feeling sick. I still believed I was right, that Cherise could not have done what she did without cheating, but it was a scandal the league did not want to pursue because integrity is everything—or the illusion of it anyway. For the first time I wondered if the skeptics were right: *was* Attitude a scam? Was the league's goal really to build a city in space? Or were we here to make a handful of players and the investors who sponsored them ungodly rich?

I changed out of my jersey, determined to go to dinner, not because I was hungry, but because I was afraid to go; afraid of what the other players would say, what they would do—and I hate being afraid.

Scents of cooked fruit and spices seeped out of the dining hall, along with a low burr of sullen conversation. I hesitated in the open doorway, staring in at a packed room. It looked like every player and every coach had come to dinner at the same time. Faces turned in my direction and the volume of conversation dropped.

I squared my shoulders and entered, weaving between the tables, all too conscious of the cold glares that followed me. And though I pretended not to hear, I was offered thoughtful advice—

"Next time play harder. You can't win by complaining."

"Even rookie stars can't win every game, Juliet. Deal with it."

"What did Cherise ever do to you?"

I kept my eyes straight ahead. Reached the buffet and filled up my plate and then wondered if there would be a place for me to sit.

Angelo rescued me. He caught my elbow, steering me to a table shared by Bruna and Min Tao, and on the way he whispered in my ear, "Guess who's not here tonight?"

I scowled at him. He returned a toothy smile. "Cherise has not come out to celebrate her victory. There's a rumor going around she's caught a mild flu."

"From where?" I asked skeptically. "Bit by a mech-skeeter?"

He shrugged. "All sorts of things come up on the space plane." As we reached the table, he pulled out a chair for me. "Dr. Kyre has ordered bed rest in her apartment. At least three days."

"Three days out of sight?"

"Exactly."

Discretion

By the next morning, I decided to do as I'd been told and go to see Cherise. I wasn't intending to apologize though; I just wanted to learn what I could about her "flu."

Skipping the lift, I took the steep stairs down to the next level, but I hesitated at the door, alerted by a faint buzzing. It was another mech-skeeter venturing up the stairwell from somewhere below. The tiny device hovered out of reach, so I turned my back on it and opened the door. It darted through to the corridor—but to my surprise it reversed course right away, and tried to return to the stairwell. I didn't let it. As it passed, I knocked it out of the air, crushing it against the floor with my foot.

I looked up to see Dr. Kyre, hesitating on his way out of one of the apartments—Cherise's apartment, I realized. He was watching me with a half smile. "We've been invaded," he said. "It happened a couple years ago too, just before the final game."

Kyre was an older man, sixty-two, a fact I knew because I'd read his profile, not because he looked it. He was the physician for Teams July, August, and September, but not for November, so I didn't know him well.

"Have you come to see my patient?" he asked. "I was told you might."

"How is she doing?" I asked, hoping my nervousness didn't show.

He spread his hands. "She's been better, but she's determined to play in the final game."

"She *is* a champion."

"I'm sure she'll welcome your company," he said, leaving the apartment door ajar.

I tapped on the door, pushed it wider, and then stepped inside. The apartment was like mine, with a tiny bathroom just inside the door, a bed beyond it, and the desk opposite, separated by a narrow strip of floor space. Cherise occupied that space, sitting in the desk chair, her feet resting on a foot stool concocted from a plastic box.

Her gaze challenged me. "I don't think you've come to apologize."

I slid the door shut. "Should I?"

As an answer she stood up. This simple movement was awkward and slow. She raised her arm. Her wrist flopped twice before she managed to hold her hand up. Watching her, a shudder of dismay ran down my spine.

"You see?" she asked. "This is what's been done to me."

So I had been right. She returned to her chair with such painful effort I wished I had been wrong. The way she sat—so stiff and motionless—it frightened me.

"You need to get treatment," I said stupidly.

"I am getting treatment." Her lips barely parted as she spoke. "Believe it or not, I'm better now than last night. Kyre swears he's treated cases like this before. He assures me it's not permanent and has promised I'll be fine by game day."

"I don't understand. Why did you—"

"I didn't do it! I didn't even suspect it. I was so angry with you for pissing on the best game I'd ever played, but as soon as I started to cool down I felt it, shooting pains in my arms and legs, a burning in my joints." She spoke with a bitterness I could easily understand. "You were right. It wasn't me playing that game. It was some jacked-up version of me."

"But how did you pass the test?"

"Cheated. Kyre did the test. He protected me."

"And the league knows that?"

"I don't know what the league knows. I just know that no one but you is asking questions, which seems very strange until you consider how much more revenue comes in if the series runs to seven games. August must have been predicted to lose, so some-one decided to help me—and so what if I got burned? I'm done anyway, right?"

I wanted to believe her, to believe she had nothing to do with it, but Cherise had her own back story. "Is it true you have an endorsement deal?"

"Oh yes. And it's also true I'll get paid a whole lot more if I help August take the championship. So . . . maybe I did this to myself?"

If she had, it was a stupid gamble—and Cherise was not stupid. "August isn't going to win Game 7 if you're not in top form."

"There won't be a Game 7 if you report me. I didn't do anything wrong, Juliet, but if this gets out, I lose everything."

"But if the A-League is involved in this—"

Her voice shot up an octave: "*No!* What is that thing doing here?" She glared at the desk, where a mech-skeeter had alighted. "I saw those in my first year."

"Min Tau thinks they're feeding information to a gambling network."

She stared at the device like it was a pile of shit, freshly fallen and steaming. "A gambling network?"

"Yes."

I smashed the skeeter so it could not betray her true condi-tion—and I hoped there were no more in the room.

Dr. Kyre must have reported my visit, because Dob Irish was out-side waiting for me when I left Cherise's room.

Yesterday, the marketer had accused me of poor sportsmanship, of lodging a frivolous protest because I was disgruntled. It was an insult that had left us mutually wary.

"It's gotten a little crazy around here," he said in an apologetic tone. "I stepped over the line yesterday. It's just that Cherise is such a popular player. For her to be . . . well, it's not just *her* public image that's been hurt."

"I'm the bad guy, right?"

His thin shoulders rose in a half-hearted shrug as a mech-skeeter glided between us. "There's work to do to repair your image."

I didn't answer this, allowing him to move on to what was really on his mind. "Were you able to discuss the cheating incident with Cherise?"

I wondered how much he knew. "The league has stated there was no cheating incident."

"And ... do you agree with that?"

He was fishing for a statement.

I resolved to give him one. "I was mistaken. Cherise did not cheat."

He smiled and nodded, knowing he could spin that handful of words to everyone's advantage. "Misunderstandings have to be expected when emotions run high."

"And still, integrity is everything—"

"Absolutely."

"—no matter how many millions of euros are riding on the outcome of this game."

His smile collapsed into a dark glare. "I'll edit that out and release the rest. It'll help, but you need to consider what you can do to salvage your image, or I'll be writing a negative assessment of your marketing potential for next year."

Like everyone else on staff, Dob received a flat salary. I wondered: had he begun to believe he deserved a little more?

Don't Ever Get Complacent

Things had gotten crazy, but I was still expected to work my shift.

It was a surreal truth that hundreds of millions of euros—maybe a billion—would be in play with the last game, but we were still working stiffs, putting in our hours on the construction and maintenance of Stage One. That was one of the marketing draws of Attitude athletes. We were sold as unassuming superstars who worked hard all week just like our fans. The only difference, we got to enjoy a little glory on game day.

The assignment that day was mundane. The space plane had

just docked and I was on a team assigned to unload construction materials, brought up at enormous cost.

Immense sums of money, forever swirling around us.

I suited up along with Bruna, Min Tao, and three others from November. I didn't tell them about my visit to Cherise. I was no attorney, but I was fairly sure I had an obligation to report what Cherise had told me. By keeping quiet, I'd become part of a conspiracy to hide the truth and I didn't want to include my friends in that.

With Min Tao and Bruna, I squeezed into the airlock, our faces hidden behind the reflective gold sheen of our visors. The inner door closed and sealed.

When we first trained to go outside we were warned, *Don't ever get complacent.*

Always, we followed procedure.

I hooked my tether to a wall loop and then reported to the gate marshal: "Secured and ready for depressurization."

"Secured," Min echoed. "Also ready."

And then Bruna, "Secured and squared away. Let's go."

"Status affirmed," the gate marshal answered. "Commencing depressurization."

My suit inflated as air was evacuated from the lock, but even in vacuum, the finely engineered joints slid with mechanical ease.

"Suit pressures steady," the gate marshal intoned. "Oxygen levels nominal. Are there any anomalies to report?"

We responded in turn, "Negative. All's well."

"Egress approved."

I turned the manual lock, pushed the door aside, and then took a moment to admire the view: Earth looming above us as night reached the mid-Pacific, with a tiny gleam of golden lights marking the islands that were my first home.

Reaching outside, I hooked a second tether into a track ring. "Secure on two."

"Release on one," the gate marshal answered. "Transferring you to the shift marshal's control."

The shift marshal acknowledged the transfer as my first tether automatically released, leaving me free to transit outside.

The space plane was docked to the core, illuminated by artificial lights. Passengers exited through a gate, but construction materials were offloaded directly from the depressurized hold, its doors standing open, the interior illuminated by docking lights. Inside was a precisely fitted row of cargo containers. Our task was to connect each to a sled that would extract it and ferry it to an assigned construction site.

Min Tao and Bruna followed me outside.

I should have proceeded directly to the sled rack, but I was distracted by a faint, whining buzz, both familiar and mysterious. My heart rate ramped up. Was something wrong with my suit?

Within the bubble of my helmet I turned my head, trying to locate the source of the sound, and as I did the buzzing grew louder until, to my shock, a mech-skeeter flew in front of my face. It bounced off the smooth curve of my visor, then landed on my lip. In instinctive panic, I shook my head, sending the device humming away, to buzz somewhere unreachable, behind my ear.

I announced my dilemma on a general channel. "There's a mech-skeeter in my suit!"

"I've got one too," Bruna said in disgust.

But we couldn't go back inside, because the other half of our offloading team was still in the airlock, and before the lock finished its cycle, two of them realized they shared our predicament. The gate marshal readmitted them, while Bruna and I were forced to wait, me with a mechanical insect walking up the back of my neck.

I was paying attention to that, not to Min Tao, when he announced, "I'm going to go ahead and do the inventory."

He kicked off toward the space plane's cargo hold, his tether extending behind him—and I looked away.

"Hey!" Bruna said. "Min Tao, why did you unhook?"

"I didn't! My tether snapped!"

I looked up, startled by the fear in his voice. I looked around, but I couldn't see him. So I pushed off the wall, pivoting until I glimpsed him as he vanished into an inky shadow beneath the space plane. Clumsy in the suit, he'd missed his jump, and now only the trailing end of his loose tether remained in the light.

"Bruna, make sure my tether doesn't slip!"

I launched myself after him with all the velocity I could generate, catching the end of his tether just before it glided out of reach.

We cycled back through the lock to a warm reception. Min Tao was mugged by our three teammates and they tried to mug me, but Dob Irish—as happy as anyone—was there too. As I got my helmet off, he pulled me away.

"Brilliant!" he whispered so only I could hear. "You handled that perfectly. Your name is already trending, and you're regaining audience sympathy."

I grabbed his arm with my thick glove, icy cold from being outside. "What are you talking about? You're not saying that was a setup? Just to boost my image?"

Dob looked annoyed. "Come on. If it was real, then Min Tao—" He frowned, thinking it over, while a mech-skeeter passed above our heads.

Behind me I heard the laughing voices of my teammates.

If I'd missed grabbing the loose tether, maybe Bruna could have gone after Min Tao with a sled, I don't know. But thinking about it, I started to shake. I imagined him floating alone out there, faced with a slow death when his air ran out—and my grip on Dob's arm tightened. "Tell me what's going on."

He shook his head, looking stricken. "It must have been an accident."

Or the A-League had betrayed us, betrayed Min Tao, betrayed Cherise, to feed a tabloid narrative designed to boost our ratings and our revenue. If so, I intended to be on the space plane when it returned to Earth.

I wriggled out of the cumbersome suit.

"Hey," Bruna said, "we still have to unload the plane."

"Check with the gate marshal. If she lets you outside before there's an investigation, then we all need to resign right now and go home."

A transit pod was already in the cradle when I reached the Spoke-1 gate. I climbed in, followed by a mech-skeeter, which settled on the transparent canopy just out of my reach. I wanted to crush it, an outlet for my anger at all that had happened, but I'd have to take off my harness to do it, so I reached for the button to close the door instead.

"Hold the pod!" a man shouted. "One more coming!"

And Dr. Kyre tumbled in with a grin.

His eyes widened as if he was surprised to find me there. "Juliet! I heard what happened outside."

He pulled himself into the seat beside me and strapped in, while the mech-skeeter decided to leave, gliding out just ahead of the closing door. It was the second time I'd seen one retreat when Kyre showed up; the first had been outside Cherise's room.

"I'm getting worried," Kyre said. "Real worried. What happened to Cherise was about ensuring a seven-game championship. What happened to Min Tao—" He pursed his lips, frowning at Earth's glittering nightside floating overhead. "I think you were right. Irish set Min Tao up."

"You talked to Irish?"

"It's the money," Kyre said in soft concern. "It makes people crazy. You need to keep that in mind, Juliet. You need to be careful."

We docked and locked and the doors opened. A group of Team August players was waiting for the pod, all of them dressed for practice. Dr. Kyre smiled, greeting each by name as he got out. I slipped past him, forgotten, and grateful for it.

Face Off

I'd never been to our CEO's office before; I'd never had cause. I was surprised to find it defended by a middle-aged receptionist who I knew to be Zaid Hackett's wife.

"I need to see her," I said.

We did the dance:

"She's busy."

"This is important."

"If you make an appointment—"

"I need to see her now."

"She's in a phone conference."

"Min Tao could have died."

That got her attention. She went to the office door, slid it open a few centimeters, and peered inside. "Zaid? Juliet Alo is here."

I was allowed in.

Zaid was seated at a desk, a fierce scowl on her face as she talked onscreen with a man I recognized as the station's chief engineer. "Of course, I agree!" she said. "Absolutely. All work outside stops until we find out what happened. Sid, I need to talk to someone. I'll check in with you in a few minutes."

The screen shifted to neutral as she turned to me. "Dob Irish thinks you and Min Tao might have manufactured the incident outside."

A mech-skeeter floated past, and then another. I sat down in the guest chair without being asked. "Integrity is everything. Was that always a lie?"

Her expression, already dark, grew ominous. "Did you manufacture the incident, or not?"

"I did not."

"But you falsely accused Cherise Caron."

"You should visit Cherise Caron."

Zaid studied me . . . and looked less certain. "I was in Paris when the scandal broke. I came up on the next flight. Haven't been here an hour." She frowned at her monitor, then at me. "I think you should tell me what's been going on."

I heard the door open behind me, and turned. Zaid's wife was there, peering in through a narrow gap. "Now Dr. Kyre is here. He says it's urgent."

I shook my head at Zaid.

She looked suddenly tired. "Not now, Helma. Thank you." As the door slid shut, she touched her monitor. "Security to my office now, please."

I rose in alarm, but Zaid waved me back to my seat. "Kyre can be . . . insistent. And I want to hear what you have to say. So speak."

"You first, ma'am. I asked a question. I need an answer."

Her lips came together in an angry line. Zaid Hackett had the respect of the world, and yet here I was, a first-year player, calling her out. Maybe she saw the irony, because she sighed and leaned back in her chair.

"Our house is in disorder. We've come to see even millions of euros as trivial, forgetting that money represents the labor of thousands of people. Real people with real lives."

"Yes, ma'am."

"What we're doing here matters, Juliet. It is *not* about the money. It's about what the money can build." She gestured at the ceiling. "This great monument, a hopeful experiment, and only the first stage of what will come. So to answer your question, integrity *is* everything. It has to be, to survive the long term, and I intend that what we build here should last for the long term. Now please, tell me what's gone wrong."

Kyre had his audience after me. I don't know what was discussed.

I was called back to my shift to help deploy a mesh around the space plane—an extra layer of safety while the cargo containers were unloaded—and after that I went to practice, worried that nothing would be done.

But I was wrong.

Two days later the space plane returned, bringing with it a team of three investigators. They questioned both players and staff, rumors ran wild, but it was the mech-skeeters that provided the critical testimony: it turned out that all the data collected by the ubiquitous little devices left the station through Dr. Kyre's account. Unknown to Cherise, her agent was paying him to make sure Team August took the championship.

The cause of Min Tao's accident could not be decisively proven, but with Kyre gone, we all feel safe again.

Cherise and I both endured a brief hearing in which our actions were examined and, ultimately, excused. She lost her endorsement contract, but she's confident she'll get another, especially if Team August takes Game 7.

As much as I admire her, it's my job to make sure that doesn't happen.

We face off tomorrow.

I intend to win.

Devil in the Dust

I'm Lance Engineer Ellie Asano, twenty-nine years old. Earth years. We don't count in Martian years. We're not here to stay. Not forever, though our five year term of service started to feel like forever when we were six months in.

I dropped in during the early days—threat-level searing red—the height of the festivities. That first year, casualties had been high, but we learned. We adapted faster than the RaVNs. And we knocked them back hard.

By the time Pold joined us, popular talk said the war was over. Martian Command had cooled the threat-rating to a barely simmering yellow: *maintain situational awareness; hostilities unlikely.* A logical inference.

Human activity served as a magnet for RaVNs; their territory had always tracked and encompassed ours. Yet my engineering team had not engaged in a firefight in over a year, and nine months had passed since the last time any team had encountered a RaVN swarm. So maybe the RaVNs *had* been defeated. Maybe they'd been wiped out.

I wanted to believe that, but I'd seen too much. No one on our rover was ready to accept that the RaVNs were done with us—especially not Pold.

There were four of us in the rover: me, Lance Engineer Kai Tussy, Sergeant Engineer Jen Haden, and Pold—aka Captain Leopold Binn, Resistance Army—technically a civilian, but a war hero, a veteran of the conflict on Earth, retired now and pulling social points as an embedded journalist, riding with us to observe the day-to-day operations of a well-construction team.

He'd been with us three days and I didn't like him.

No, that's not true.

I didn't *want* to like him.

My team had only two months to go before our scheduled return to real life on Earth and like all short-timers, we were jumpy. Hyper-wary, hyper-alert, flinching at any hint of movement in the dust, absolutely determined not to die in that wind-blown hell. Too many ghosts there already, howling past the pressure seals.

As we'd rolled out of mobile base 12, Haden and Kai in the cab, me and Pold together in the mess, I'd warned him, "We are going to do all we can to avoid excitement on this trip. It would be too tragic to die now, at the end of the struggle."

His response had shocked me. "No one should have died here." Dark cynicism freighted his low voice as he went on, "Your presence here is propaganda. It always has been."

When you've been in the dust for years, seen so many good people die, it's hard to hear someone declare it all for nothing—especially when that judgment comes from someone you wanted to respect. I argued with Pold, it got heated between us, but no way was he going to change his mind. Despite his war experience—hell, because of it—he did not believe in the core mission.

"The duty statement is bullshit," he insisted. "You don't need to be here. You don't need to die here. No one does. We could have beaten the RaVNs faster with swarms of our own, but the Coalition doesn't want to win that way. That strategy doesn't support the philosophy of '*Human intelligence only.*' So we send our best to role-play heroes, a human sacrifice to enforce the Coalition's founding statement—"

"That collectively we have what it takes to beat machine minds," I recited. "And we do."

"Sure. You've shown that here. You're close to beating the RaVNs. But at what cost?"

He didn't mean material resources. The true cost was human lives, blood spilled onto the dust and boiling away in the deadly low-pressure. But I didn't want to concede the point, so I executed a churlish shift in tactics.

"How many social points have you had deducted for opinions like that?" I asked him.

A sly grin—the first sign of humor I'd seen from him. "*Thousands*," he had assured me. "And I can't afford to lose anymore, so don't set me off again, okay?"

I'd hissed my non-agreement. But he *was* a war hero. Maybe he deserved the slack. I'd shrugged and assured him, "I'll do what I can."

Now we were together in the cab. The team had been driving in shifts through the night, with the goal of reaching the next equipment drop by 0800 Local. Haden and Kai were asleep in the bunks. I had the stick, with Pold in the co-pilot seat.

He didn't have the training to drive, but he had years of experience hunting RaVNs, so Haden had put him to work on day one. His job was to watch the terrain, the map, and our positions on both. From the beginning, he'd demonstrated a preternatural ability to stay alert. His attention didn't waver, and he didn't call false alarms.

In the predawn twilight I needed my NVV—night-vision visor—to negotiate the variable canyon-country terrain. The rover rolled on tall shape-shifting wheels, its chassis segmented into three parts by flexible joints that helped it get over the rough spots. The cab was all windows. We could get away with that because the artificial magnetosphere kept out the worst of the radiation. The growing atmosphere helped too—at our location, roughly the equivalent of a 15-kilometer elevation on Earth.

The view was nice to have in the daytime, but spooky in the dark. Too easy to imagine cold, silent, undetectable camera eyes watching us out of the night.

I drove slowly, studying every aspect of the approaching terrain, mentally plotting a best route. We were in a wide, shallow canyon. Our route kept us close to the northern wall, where fossilized landslides spilled onto the ancient terrain, forming steep ridges that climbed like ramps to meet the cracked cliff face. I'd been dodging rocks for an hour, so when we finally reached a thirty-meter stretch of clean, wind-scrubbed hardpan, I used the respite to reach for my water bottle.

Just as I did, Pold spoke. Two soft syllables: "D-D."

I sucked in a sharp breath. DD. Dust devil—but not the towering plumes that wandered the sun-warmed surface of the planet. Among the combat engineering teams, DD meant small-scale ambiguous motion—a devil in the dust—usually glimpsed in the periphery of your vision, leaving you praying it was a swirl of grit raised by the wind, or the contorted shadow of an aerial survey drone passing unexpectedly overhead.

We were so far from Earth, prayers like that were rarely heard, even more rarely answered.

Abandoning the water bottle, I stomped the brake, hit the alarm to waken Haden and Kai, and then pulled and turned the knob to open the roof hatch. Distantly, the *ka-chunk* of a lock releasing, clank of steel and whirr of an electric motor as a Wafer drone unfolded long fabric wings sufficient to support the weight of an array of cameras in the thin atmosphere, but nothing more.

A permitted aspect of narrow AI would keep the Wafer's wings properly trimmed for current atmospheric conditions, but the drone's default flight pattern followed a fixed protocol: a quick circle of the rover before quartering the terrain farther out, the guidance system just flexible enough to keep the Wafer away from high ridges and canyon walls.

With the Wafer up, I undertook my own survey, twisting in my seat, left to right, visually scanning a landscape made bright—almost too bright—by my NVV. Blame that on the gray edge of dawn, filtering through the Martian atmosphere.

I didn't see any RaVNs, but that only meant we weren't being swarmed—yet.

"What have you got?" I asked Pold, my voice hoarse with the ever-present dust.

Movement between us: Sergeant-Engineer Haden filling the narrow aisle. She must have benefitted from a momentary time-warp and heard the alarm before I sent it, because she appeared wide awake, her legs already sheathed in the lower half of her armored exosuit, her body twisting as she worked to get her arms inside. "Talk," she ordered.

"Initial sighting, four o'clock," Pold reported, not looking at her. Looking back instead, behind the rover, using his NVV. "Single spider. Behind us now."

"*Shit*," Haden whispered, pressing the front seam of her suit to seal it. "No EM or motion signatures?" she asked me.

"Silent and still," I reported as I cycled through feeds from the rover's external cameras. "And no alerts from the Wafer."

Lack of a signal did not mean much. Solitary RaVNs were good at evading detection.

Haden leaned in, console lights revealing her sharp, bony features, the tension in her eyes. "Find it for me, Ellie."

I wanted to, but nothing showed on my feeds, not in any wavelength. Not yet.

"You get many strays on these circuits?" Pold asked.

"Strays only happen post-combat," Haden answered. "And there's been no combat in this region for ten months. This one's a scout—and that means we've got—"

"A nest around here somewhere," Pold finished for her.

"Right. Move, both of you. Get your suits on."

I dropped my NVV into a bin on the console and released my harness. Pold was already up, squeezing past Haden when I started to rise. That's when I saw it on-screen, just for a moment, before the feed shifted to a different camera.

I tapped the screen, shifting back to the prior feed, and there it was: a mechanical daddy-long-legs, waist high, a central sphere the size of a small tangerine suspended between the inverted V's of six multi-jointed legs, so thin they were hard to see in the gray light. "Ah, fuck. Spider confirmed."

"*Move!*" Haden barked.

I moved, bailing out over the back of the seat while she took over my position. "Kai, get your ass up here."

"Right here, ma'am," he answered in his low, gravelly voice.

He wasn't kidding. I almost collided with him as I exited the cab. A big man, at least twenty centimeters taller than me, he looked even bigger fully suited with his helmet sealed, ready to play. His suit's internal struts hissed as he pushed past me. He carried Haden's helmet, issuing his own order—"Seal up, boss"—while she called in the sighting to base.

I left them to it, and darted into the mess—a misnomer if there ever was one. The place was spotless and unobstructed, table and counters folded out of the way after every meal. Five years in the dust will teach you to keep the floor clear, the rover neat. Everything in its place and nothing blocking access to the lockers.

Pold had his locker's accordion door open. He stripped off his sweater and his thermal pants, every motion smooth, practiced, efficient, peeling down to the silky red-brown fabric of his form-fitting underskin.

We all wore the skins all the time. They monitored our physiological status and tracked our movements, sharing the data with our suits—another instance of a permitted learning system.

Artificial Intelligence—even narrow AI—magnified the power of the individual controlling it. AI had allowed the global aristocracy to launch the Point One Insurrection. A billion people culled that first year, twice that lost after the RaVNs went feral.

Since then, the People's Coalition had banned AI except by permit, in narrow applications.

Pold asked, "You found my RaVN?"

I popped my own locker door. "Yeah. Spider surveyor. Probably fresh spawn and stupid or it wouldn't have come so close—but it needed to figure us out."

"Next time it'll know us by the vibration of the wheels."

"Won't be a next time."

"Right."

It started on Mars, with good intentions, when five Von Neumann swarms were released from an automated base. The swarms were a distributed intelligence, with individual components specialized to different tasks—survey work, excavation, smelting, molecular assembly, reproduction—with the potential to evolve new specialties as needed. Deep programming directed them to search out likely mineral deposits, excavate a nest, gather necessary materials, and then synthesize, print, and assemble components to create a new swarm.

Along the way, the swarms worked cooperatively at tasks ranging from assembling shelters for human colonists to constructing well sites designed to drill deep into the crust, seeking volatiles to help grow an atmosphere and ultimately raise the surface temperature.

But early in the Insurrection the swarms were hacked—by the Point One? Or by the People? No official word on that, but Mars was always a billionaires' project, so my guess is, it was one of us who tried to strike back by adapting the Von Neumann swarms to war.

Big mistake.

The Radicalized Von Neumanns—RaVNs—dropped out of communication, disappeared into underground nests, grew their numbers, and then emerged without warning. They attacked the scattered settlements. Blew holes in them. Eliminated every one. Two years later, they showed up on Earth.

Were they brought back on an uncrewed ship? Or did the Point One replicate them? I've heard both theories. What's known for sure is that on Earth, RaVNs found a home they liked. They nested in old landfills—everything they needed could be found in those neatly sculpted hills—and the heat their activities generated was undetectable beneath the heat of decay.

I saw my first swarm when I was ten. Our neighborhood was under curfew and we were supposed to stay indoors, but me and my sister were bored. We slipped outside, into the little backyard. Just a few minutes. A soft, dreamy droning made me look up. Heavy gray clouds in a cold autumn sky. Nothing else to see, not right away. Later, I understood the kamikazes were camouflaged. I will never forget my mother's shrill scream, or the skull-shaking explosion that took my sister's life.

Pold was a veteran of the war that eliminated that scourge from Earth, but we were still fighting on Mars.

I peeled down to my underskin. My exosuit hung ready in the locker. I backed in, grabbed the monkey bar, hauled myself up, and then dropped into the legs while the suit was still on the rack. Kicked clear, then shoved my arms into the sleeves. Zipped, snapped, sealed.

Pold stayed one step ahead of me. Before we'd left base, we'd made him practice suiting up, though he already knew the procedure. Earth had seen the first use of armored exosuits. They'd become necessary when the RaVNs turned to poison gas to cull human populations.

I grabbed my backpack, strapped it on. My helmet went on last—and not before I heard the mounted machine gun begin to hammer, faint concussions barely audible through the rover's insulation.

I shoved my locker door shut while confirming airflow and my radio link. "Asano, checking in," I reported over comms.

"Confirmed," Haden replied.

Pold elbowed his locker closed. "We're going after the nest, right?" he asked, his voice arriving over comms, a low, intimate vibration in my ears.

"Affirmative," Haden answered. "Core mission. *We* are going after the nest. You're staying here to watch—"

"Brace!" Kai barked.

The rover jumped and shuddered before I could take Kai's good advice. The impact tossed me off my feet. I hit the supply cabinets and stuck, Pold on top of me as a hurricane blast of depressurization incited a coordinated riot of blankets, hand-held electronics, food packets, and dust, all whipping past us, made visible by the glow of red emergency lights.

The riot of thoughts in my head was even more chaotic: the rover had flipped onto its side and ruptured, Haden was suited but she didn't have her backpack on and that meant her air supply would run out in a couple of minutes, Kai had been operating a remote machine gun but if he still had a link to it, I couldn't hear it over the storm. Oh, and we'd wandered into the neighborhood of a RaVN nest aggressive enough to take out our rover within seconds of discovery—and that only happened when a nest was ready to fledge.

"We've got to get to it!" I shouted. "We've got to burn that nest. We can't let it go."

If the nest fledged, reproductive units would be released. The RUs, each accompanied by a swarm of escorts, would scatter, speeding off in different directions to disappear, dig in, establish new nests. Kamikaze units would emerge at the same time. Those would target us, and then swarm any human-built structure they could find, from mobile bases to the microbial injection wells that we were tasked with assembling.

Pold rolled off me but stayed low, belly-crawling toward the weapons cabinet. An orange icon at the side of my visor's display indicated Kai's abnormal status, probably injured but not leaking air. Haden remained green, but that wouldn't last.

I scrambled up, standing stooped beneath lockers that now made a low ceiling. Reached up and shoved open the accordion door on Haden's locker. Only the backpack left, secured in brackets against the rear wall. I stretched to reach it and came up five centimeters short. So I jumped, taking care not to trigger an assist from my suit's exoskeleton. No mechanical help needed for this. I tapped the release and caught the backpack as it fell free.

Turning, I expected to find Haden come to retrieve her gear, but she wasn't there. I looked to the front of the rover, stunned to see the cab gone, peeled off in the explosion.

A dim scattering of dawn light illuminated the Martian landscape: wind-smoothed, lifeless grit interspersed with small stones, and farther out, the fan of an ancient landslide rising in a steep slope to meet the distant, polished face of the canyon wall.

What was going on out there? The Wafer could show me. A tap on the control panel on my left arm would link me to its video feed, but would I have the necessary seconds to study the layout? I judged not.

I scrambled forward, hauling Haden's pack, expecting the rover to be hit again. I needed to be clear before that happened—but it wouldn't do me any good to get outside if I wasn't armed. So I spent a few seconds to raid the already-open weapons cabinet.

Pold must have pulled a gun for Haden as well as himself, because only one rifle remained. I took it, along with an ammo pack and the two explosives satchels. As I did, I spoke, "Am I clear to exit?" Suddenly aware of my rapid breathing, the runaway hammer of my heart.

To my deep relief, Haden answered, her words soft and short to conserve her air. "Clear. *Move.*"

In that last syllable, an unspoken command, *Get my air over here now.* We had served together three years.

I bounded out into a debris field made up of artifacts that had been inside our rover until seconds ago.

A quick look around showed me canyon floor to my right, with dust drifted up against boulders and fragments of the rover resting at the end of impact trails. Farther up the canyon, Pold lay behind a ripple of dune, the binocular sight of his rifle pressed against his faceplate. On my left, upside down and at an angle to the rest of the rover, was the cab, neatly severed at the articulated joint.

Haden stood within the scant shelter of the cab's glass walls. She had her rifle slung on her shoulder as she worked to lower Kai from an upside-down seat.

With an assist from my exosuit, I jumped to meet her. A single bound put me at her side. I dropped her pack. Laid the weapons down with more care, keeping their muzzles out of the dust. Haden had already freed Kai from his harness. I helped her ease him to the ground.

As soon as he was down, I told her, "Grab your air."

She complied, scrambling to her pack, getting herself hooked up to an air supply. *Secure yourself first, then your mates.*

I heard the gasping intake of her breath. "Ah, that's better," she sighed.

From Kai, a faint moan as I lowered his slack body to the ground. He'd seen it coming, called out a warning before the blast hit on his side of the rover. His armor was dented and blackened, his visor spiderwebbed. Blood bubbled from three pinpoints before crystallizing in swiftly growing rings of red ice. I couldn't see through to his face, but his icon remained orange, which was a step above red, and an infinite distance above black.

"I'm pulling your bivouac sack," Haden warned, a moment before I felt a tug on my pack.

Precious seconds expended as we unfolded it, moved Kai onto it, and sealed him inside the transparent material.

"Pold, what do you see?" Haden asked as we worked.

"Sand crab. Ducked behind cover. It's trying to wait me out."

"That's what hit us," I growled.

Sand crabs were stealth kamikazes. Their protocol was to scurry under a rover, jump to attach at a vulnerable joint, and then trigger the explosives they carried. They usually came in threes, so there was likely another that Pold hadn't spotted yet.

"Seen the spider again?" Haden asked him.

"Nope."

I flinched at the sound of a gunshot, picked up by my external mic.

"Got it," Pold reported.

Two seconds later, an explosion, tinny in the ultra-thin air as the disabled 'kazi triggered its load.

If the rule of threes held, one more 'kazi sand crab remained. The elusive spider was out there too, out of sight. It wouldn't attack, but only watch, reporting our activities to the nest.

We needed to find that nest. It would be underground, the entrance would be concealed, and by this time, outgoing comms would have been silenced, so it wasn't going to be easy to locate, even with the Wafer hunting for it.

Using the bivouac sack's grab handles, Haden and I hefted Kai as gently as we could, and carried him away from the wreck of the rover.

"Over here," Haden directed.

We laid him behind sheltering stone. I inflated the sack. It was designed to disguise his heat signature, making him harder for wandering RaVNs to sense, but it would offer no protection if one found him. I hated to leave him, but we had to get the nest.

"Hey, Kai, you hear me?" I asked.

Faintly, "*Yeah.*"

"Lay quiet," Haden ordered him. "Emergency transmissions only."

"Get 'em, boss," he whispered.

"We will."

We couldn't report our situation to mobile base—we were too far out in the dust for direct contact and with the cab wrecked we couldn't reach a satellite relay—but Haden had already called in the sighting, so mobile base was alerted. And when the rover failed its automated all-systems-nominal report, issued at five-minute intervals, the roo jumpers would scramble, bringing in the big guns.

Still, given our distance from mobile, we'd probably be on our own for most of an hour. Time enough for a mature nest to rush final preparations.

Nests were smart. This one would understand that to fledge successfully, it would have to act now. Soldier swarms were surely being prepped to come after us, tasked with keeping us engaged in a hot defense to buy the necessary minutes the reproductive units needed to power up and acquire wings.

If even one reproductive swarm slipped away, the war could go on, maybe for years.

Pold went out on his own to search the ground around the blown-up sand crab, so he was first to find an indication of the nest's location.

"Tracks," he reported. "Too faint for the Wafer to see. They come from over this ridge ahead of the rover."

He stood at the base of a slope of grit and boulders—a massive landslide that had sagged from the canyon wall in some ancient epoch to form a ridge almost a kilometer long. On the wall above the ridge, a deep cleft. A prime nest site, if ever I saw one.

The circling Wafer had already imaged the immediate area. I called up a projection onto my visor's display. Rotated it to see into the cleft. No hotspots showed in infrared, and in visible light the cleft appeared as a black gash, filled with inky shadows.

"Follow the tracks, Ellie," Haden said. "Tell me what you see. I'm going around the ridge to get a look ahead."

She bounded away, while I hurried to catch up with Pold. Motion sensors in my helmet watched both ground and sky, ready to bleat an alarm if they sensed activity, but I didn't rely on them. Sand crabs knew how to lie in wait, so I kept a close eye on the ground around me.

"Tracks confirmed," I reported when I caught up to Pold. The marks were faint and fading swiftly in the wind, but there was no doubt the sand crab had made them. "The trail leads up and over the ridge. I'm on it."

"Confirmed," Haden said. "I'll cover from below."

She was already a tiny figure, and still only a quarter of the way to the end of the ridge.

I started to climb, using the power of my exosuit to advance in swift bounds as I followed the wispy tracks. Even with assistance, my heart rate ramped up, my breathing chuffed in my ears.

Pold followed at a slower pace, still a stranger to Martian gravity.

After a minute, I lost the trail, but I didn't want to backtrack. There wasn't time, and I was sure the nest couldn't be far. I worried that the Wafer hadn't found any sign of the entrance yet, but the lack of alarms also assured me the nest remained quiet. No RUs had tried to fledge so far.

"Why did they hit us?" Pold asked over comms, speaking between breaths. "Smarter, to let us pass unhindered. Stay hidden. Keep the secret of their nest. Fledge and reproduce and build up their numbers. That's how Earth swarms operated."

"Shh," I hissed. "Don't let 'em know that."

He persisted. "It's a question of resources, isn't it? A lot scarcer here than on Earth."

Haden answered before I could, breathing easily despite her pace. "That's right. The RaVNs here are driven by mixed imperatives—attack, reproduce, fledge. They need the right substrates to reproduce and the raw materials aren't so easy to find here. So they learned to follow the vibration of machinery, the scent of metals in the well towers. And it works for them. We can't guard every installation."

"They take risks," I panted. "We do too." Maybe I was taunting Pold.

"So yes," Haden continued. "It would have been smarter for this nest to lie low. But RaVNs can't escape their core programming."

"And neither can we," he added grimly, just as a helmet alarm went off.

The alarm wasn't mine; it came over comms. I dropped into a crouch, already three hundred meters above the canyon floor. Haden had crouched too, a tiny figure near the end of the ridge.

"*Shit*," she whispered. "That's Kai's motion alarm."

Meaning something had found him. The spider? Or a 'kazi?

I swallowed hard. Stood up. Resumed climbing. "It's on you, boss. I'm too high to drop back now, and Pold's too slow."

"*Shit*," she said again, this time with an inflection of agreement. "Do what you have to do, Ellie. Find that nest. Kill it."

"Yes, ma'am."

Far below, her small figure running, racing back to Kai.

"You with me, Pold?" I asked.

"Getting the hang of it, ma'am." And then he added, "You promised me no excitement."

"Ah, hell, I knew you needed the social points."

I was almost to the crest of the ridge, when Pold said, "Pepper swarm. Two o'clock. Visual in ten."

I listened, but my external mic only picked up the crunch of gravel under my boots and the ethereal wind. "You hear it?" I asked skeptically.

"I can see the EM as a golden haze."

"*Fuck*." He was augmented.

"Yeah. Halfway to the enemy, huh?"

Augmentation wasn't permitted anymore, but I guess it was still acceptable in the war's opening days. The idea of Pold being augmented gave me the creeps, but it impressed me, too.

The Wafer, lagging Pold by several seconds, finally picked up the swarm, bleating an alarm just as my mic captured a familiar fierce buzz. I dropped against the slope, rolled to face the sky, and raised my weapon as the pepper swarm came over the ridge— black grains scattered against gray sky. They were aerial kamikazes, equipped with just enough explosive to punch holes in things. I counted ten, so high overhead I knew they weren't after me. I wanted to launch a grenade in among them, but they were out of range.

Bam!

I flinched at the soft concussion of a distant explosion, almost inaudible over the rush of my breathing and the buzz of the swarm.

"Haden!" I demanded as the peppers sped away toward the ruined rover. "You okay? You got the 'kazi?"

"Kazi 3 is down," Haden confirmed in sharp-edged syllables. "Kai is unmolested."

"Kazi called for help," I warned her. "Peppers passed us, looking for you."

"Get to the nest!" she snapped. "Go, go, go!"

My mind flashed on the spider, hunkered down somewhere, watching us, watching me, relaying what it saw to the intelligence that was the nest. Our window of opportunity could not last much longer.

I got up, bounded the rest of the way to the crest of the ridge, whispering profanities as my external mic picked up a chorus of distant pepper-pops, carried on a ghost wind.

The shadowed cleft in the canyon wall was now just a hard scrabble away across a few meters of near-vertical rock. The Wafer hadn't found any sign of activity up there, but its wingspan didn't allow it to enter the cleft. To know for sure if the nest was there or not, I'd have to go in myself.

I plotted a route in my mind and started to climb. Right away, I slipped, as the ancient stone gave out under my weight. I caught myself, heart racing, skin clammy with a cold sweat, and started again. That's when Pold finally reached the crest of the ridge.

"Stop, Ellie," he said softly. "The action is below us."

I glanced down past my boot. *Shit*, it was a long way! But I couldn't see anything to indicate the presence of a nest down there. "Not seeing it," I growled. "And the Wafer doesn't see anything either."

"I *do*."

He didn't stay to argue. Instead, he vaulted from the top of the ridge, dropping at least eighteen meters, then sliding another three or four before arresting his momentum. From there, he continued down, angling toward the canyon wall . . . where I saw, to my chagrin, a stream of peppers pouring from beneath a concealing shelf of rock.

The RaVNs had left no debris apron to give away the location of the nest entrance, but the swarming peppers served as an unmistakable arrow pointing back to its location.

"Hit it!" I screamed at Pold, aborting my climb to scramble after him.

All we had to do was close the entrance, containing the reproductive units in their underground lair until the roo jumpers arrived with explosives that would collapse the nest and crush every RaVN trapped inside.

"I haven't got the angle," Pold told me.

The peppers lofted into the sky, following each other in such tight formation they looked like a flying snake. Two triplets of 'kazi sand crabs emerged next from beneath the overhang, sprinting toward Pold on their four articulated legs, their flattened carapaces tinted in a burnt and faded shade of red to match the grit.

"Ah, fuck," Pold said in eloquent summary.

I shouldered my weapon and fired a grenade at the sand crabs just as they started to scatter. A geyser of dust and grit and spinning robot legs fountained into the air. No secondary explosions followed. That might mean some were too disabled to self-trigger, but it wasn't likely I'd gotten them all.

Pold had dropped flat to dodge the shrapnel. Now, from the corner of my eye, I saw the pepper swarm converging on him. He rolled. A grenade rocketed from the muzzle of his weapon, exploding among the peppers. Shrapnel knocked half of them to the ground. The concussion destabilized the rest, but in the ultra-thin atmosphere the pressure wasn't enough to cause damage and they quickly recovered.

Motion drew my eye away, to a surviving sand crab scrambling toward Pold. Not a surprise. The soldiers never retreated. They were made for sacrifice, replaceable parts in an entity comprised of the entire RaVN flight.

I shifted triggers and put two short bursts into the kamikaze. That action drew the surviving peppers away from Pold. They swiftly assembled, snaking through the air toward my position. Pold seized the chance, jumping up and racing toward the nest.

I pumped a grenade into the pepper swarm and then aimed my weapon at the ground ahead of Pold, pressing my visor against the rifle's fitted scope, hunting for any surviving kamikazes in his path.

I saw one. He saw it too and threw himself to the side. I took my shot, but the 'kazi beat me. It self-triggered as Pold rolled down the slope. The blast spewed shrapnel. It mostly missed him.

Mostly.

Pold gasped, swore. Then he came up onto a knee, erupting in a furious tirade: "This is a stupid way to fight!" He got his feet under him, staggered back up the slope, his breathing harsh enough that I could hear it over comms, but he kept shouting. "The only reason we're here is because the Coalition wants heroes. Manufactured heroes! That's what this is about. That's all it's about."

He would have been better off saving his breath. Same for me. But as I headed down, scrambling, sliding, leaving deep scars in the dust, I shouted back, "No! It's about beating the RaVNs! That's what it's about!"

"You think we have to fight this way? We *don't*. I used to supervise an autonomous swarm."

No way did I believe that. I did not *want* to believe it. He was a decorated war hero, he'd helped to exterminate the RaVNs from Earth—and now he wanted me to believe that he and his cohorts had needed to adopt enemy tactics, that the Coalition's human forces could not do it on their own.

"That's bullshit," I said. "Human forces defeated the RaVNs on Earth."

"Yeah, that's what they want you to believe." Speaking softly now.

He'd reached the level of the nest. Twenty meters away, the cliff face: rough and ragged, a wind-sculpted tangle of stone.

I came down a few meters behind him. Looked for the nest entrance. I couldn't see it. But he could—or maybe he only saw the golden glow of microwave communications emanating from it. Whatever it was, he fired from the hip, another grenade, just as two surviving peppers dropped out of the sky. Both went off, their blast zones intercepting the grenade. Two small pops and one emphatic *boom!* accompanied by a brilliant flash. Grit pelted my visor and a cloud of dust billowed among the rocks.

Pold was on the ground, face-down. At first, I thought he'd dropped to dodge the shrapnel, but he didn't try to get up again. He didn't stir at all.

Shit.

I wanted to check on him, but the nest came first.

And anyway, we were both replaceable.

I bounded past him and plunged into the dust cloud, imagining RaVNs in their subterranean haunts, sensing the vibration of my steps, tracking my approach, putting a defensive unit together to meet me.

I cut around a screen of rock. Behind it, I found a jagged fissure in the canyon wall, less than a meter wide, light from above indicating it was an extension of the larger cleft I'd tried to reach from the ridge top. Twelve meters in, I could see its back wall. At the foot of that wall, a lightless half-oval opening, not even knee-high. Emerging from the opening, a swarm of sand crab kamikazes, racing on articulated legs to meet me—and there was more movement behind them. An undefined shape in the darkness.

Easy to guess what that was. The nest had to be desperate to fledge. A reproductive swarm would emerge next—the first of many. Ten, twenty, possibly a hundred depending on how long this nest had been gestating, how successful its foraging had been.

I needed to close the entrance now. No reproductive units could escape. I couldn't let that happen. For Pold, for Haden, for Kai—for all the ghosts haunting the dust—I needed this to end, now.

All this swirling thought, contained within a moment—and then I reacted.

Five years in the dust had taught me how to work the gravity and use the mechanical boost of my exosuit. I crouched, and then, with the charging 'kazis already halfway through the cleft, I jumped.

I jumped high, catching myself with gloves and boots against the jagged stone, balancing there, suspended as the kamikazes passed beneath me and continued on, out the mouth of the cleft. The action I'd just taken was outside the perimeter of their understanding. They did not know where I had gone.

I kicked off the wall toward the entrance. Landed in a rolling crouch, came up on my knees, grit crunching and a swirl of red-brown dust stirred up by the buzzing rotor of the first reproductive unit to emerge from the nest.

The unit started to lift. I flipped my rifle around and swung it. Brought the stock down hard. Did it again, hammering the RU into stillness. Then I jumped to my feet and kicked the wreckage back toward the nest as a second unit crept into sight. At the same time, I wrestled one of the explosive satchels from my thigh pocket.

My external mic picked up the blast of a doubled explosion not far behind me, but I didn't take the time to look. There was only the mission. I kicked the two RUs back underground, then dropped again to my knees. Toggled the satchel on. Shoved it into the dark as far as I could reach.

A robot could have done this job.

No one had spoken, but the thought came to me as if someone had whispered it into my mind.

A smart, cheap, replaceable robot.

I jumped up, turned. Ran as hard as I knew how. Not slowing at all when I registered the presence of a tall dark shape blocking my escape from the cleft.

I trusted Pold to step out of the way.

He did, waving me on. "*Run!* Get out of here! This whole fissure is gonna collapse."

He was probably right.

I skidded past the concealing screen of rock, Pold a step behind me. We scrambled along the side of the ridge, angling for the crest, trying to put distance behind us and to get over the top.

I felt the shudder of the explosion through my boots. Then the shockwave, like the ghost of a hurricane—but the shrapnel bit with sharp teeth in the back of my thighs and rattled against my helmet. My suit alarm howled that I had a breach, I needed to patch. Behind us, the canyon wall, coming down.

I thought I heard Haden demanding to know my status but it was hard to be sure given the bone-shaking rumble of avalanche.

Later, I asked Pold, "Is it true what you said, about an autonomous swarm?"

I kept my voice low. We weren't alone. The roo jumpers had arrived just over an hour after the initial attack on our rover. They'd conducted a quick survey of the canyon, then set up a survival tent, moving us into it.

That part was a blur for me. I was pretty beat up. We all were. Kai had a nasty concussion, me and Haden had frostbite and vacuum damage, Pold did too, along with deep tissue bruising.

But we'd succeeded in closing the nest, and the roo jumpers had drilled shafts, dropping enough explosives into them to collapse any remaining tunnels. Now we were just waiting for a rover to come pick us up.

Pold lay on the air mattress next to mine, staring up at the tent's canopy. "No," he said, in answer to my question, his voice a hoarse whisper. "I shouldn't have said that. It was a lie."

I sighed and lay back, wanting to believe him, willing to do so.

But Haden had overheard this exchange and knew what we were talking about. She'd heard it all over comms. She propped herself up on an elbow, looked at me past Kai's bulk—he was asleep—and told me, "Shut up about it. It's classified."

"*Shit*," I whispered, because that meant it was true. The Coalition *had* used autonomous swarms to combat the RaVNs on Earth, violating our own founding statement.

Haden didn't want us talking about it. We could lose social points that way. But Pold lived by his own rules.

"There wasn't a choice," he said in a low voice just above a whisper. "We had to use swarms to fight swarms. No other way. The RaVNs were too numerous, too widespread. Living in landfills, junkyards, abandoned industrial sites, reproducing faster than we could knock them back. Here, the life cycle is slower. Necessary elements are hard to find. But even here, it's taken twelve years and thousands of living breathing irreplaceable human souls."

That thought again: *A robot could have done this job.*

I shook my head—gently, because it hurt—rejecting the statement. Not because it was untrue, but because it was dangerous.

"It was hard," I conceded. "It was costly, but in the end, we did it. We proved it could be done—and without violating the founding statement. That *matters*. If we go back to the way it was, hand off all the hard tasks to machines, then we, the people, will be right back where we were when autonomous systems allowed a few people to murder billions. That magnification of power, that's what we can't afford."

Silence, stretching through seconds.

"We're fragile," Pold said at last. "Recognize that. It never mattered much to me when I lost components in the swarms I supervised. I just requisitioned replacements. But there's no way to replace the soldiers who died because the defensive swarms were banned, who lost their lives for an arbitrary political decision."

"We're past that now," Haden said gently. "We've said no to dehumanization. Now we're moving forward, learning to trust ourselves again, to convince ourselves we *can* do this, if we work together."

I closed my eyes, hearing the wind outside the tent, the voices of ghosts lost in the dust.

Just like me, they longed for home.

—⁓—

Region Five

I WAS A soldier not a human fly, but Trident swore the battle AI could make it work. My helmet's audio quieted the sounds of shouts and screams and gunfire from the streets below, and the rumble of helicopters above the city, so that it was easy for me to hear Trident as he spoke over a private channel from his post at the Guidance office in Charleston: "You've got to trust me, Josh. We've got a viable route for you. But it's only going to work if you move out when I call it. No hesitation."

I wondered when we'd gotten to a first-name basis. Trident was the lieutenant's remote handler, but the lieutenant was dead in a checkpoint blast that had been just one in a simultaneous wave of attacks that brought our peacekeeping efforts to an abrupt end.

It had been "Sergeant Miller" when Trident first opened a persistent link with my helmet's audio, informing me of what I already knew: that I was now in command of my Linked Combat Squad. *We'll work together*, he'd told me. *I'll help you get out of there.* That was thirty minutes ago, as a guerilla army of RPs poured up out of the subway tunnels, and barricades were going up in the streets. Time enough for our relationship to get tight—but I didn't like what he was asking me to do next.

Asshole, I thought, but I focused a little too hard on the sentiment. My wired skullcap picked up the cerebral pattern, my tactical AI interpreted it, and a synthesized voice spoke the thought for me in a flat artificial tone that went out over the persistent channel linking me to Trident. "Asshole," it said.

"Oops," I added out loud.

Trident took it well. "You just need to get the squad to the roof, Josh."

"I understand the goal." I just didn't like the route.

I was crouched on the edge of an abyss, behind a concrete pillar that had once framed the now-blown-out glass wall of an office suite on the thirty-eighth floor of an eighty-eight story skyscraper designated as building 21-North. The suite was a temporary refuge for my LCS—my Linked Combat Squad. Fifteen soldiers, twelve of us still alive. We'd set up booby traps to be triggered by the battle AI when the door was inevitably breached. Of course we planned to be gone by then.

I looked past glittering fragments of shattered glass at a forest of high-rise buildings, a hundred or more: the once-affluent city center of Region Five. Scattered fires billowed and blazed in offices that had been hit by rocket fire, and black smoke from burning cars wended up from the street, poisoning the air between the buildings.

Beyond the towers, just visible through the smoke, were the mixed districts. Green marked the gated neighborhoods with their large parks and luxury homes; gray was the color of the ugly, low-rise concrete block apartments that served as middle-class housing; and sealing the spaces between them—like multicolored mold—were the slums. A vast, interconnected maze of tumble-down homes that sprawled all the way to the glittering airport, ten miles out.

The airport was our goal, our destination. Home base. Safety in a region gone mad, and it was my task to get my LCS there before the RPs got to us. But car bombs and barricades had closed the roads out of the city center, and snipers held posts in most of the buildings, waiting to pick off any foreign soldier unwise enough to set foot in the streets. So Command had decided that our only way out was up.

I felt pressure on my shoulder. Turned to see Kat's hand, inside an armored glove. Leaning down, she asked off-com: "How long we gonna' be here, Sergeant?" Her voice crisp, calm, reflecting the focused state of her baseline mood.

"Not long. We'll be going as soon as the route is clear."

We'd decimated the crew of RPs that had followed us up the stairwell, but there would be more. We didn't call them "Replacement Parts" for nothing. RPs were shock troops drawn from the slums, the expendable weapons of a warlord who crapped in gold-plated toilets while he claimed to be fighting for the poor. RP training was minimal, but they came in such numbers and jacked up so high on designer drugs it hardly mattered. We'd probably killed thirty or more, just getting into 21-North. I hoped their signing bonus was worth it.

Kat dropped into a crouch beside me. "Busy out there," she observed, still off-com so the rest of the squad wouldn't hear her.

"Robot war," I agreed, answering the same way as we watched a pair of cheap kamikazes dart past in the gulf below us. They were small UAVs—four-foot wingspans, electric engines, propeller driven—fast and agile. They peeled off, heading in opposite directions down an adjacent avenue.

Trident had sworn that we'd won the initial air war. Enemy UAVs had been eliminated while we climbed the tower, and anything still in flight belonged to us. Maybe it was true.

I flinched as another kamikaze dropped out of the sky. It shot past us in a dive so steep I thought it was aimed at a target in the street. But fifteen or twenty floors below our position, it shifted its trajectory, pulling up, and then accelerating through a shattered window in the building across the street. Red flames ballooned at the point of impact.

"You know why this city is code-named Region Five?" Kat asked.

"Not sure I want to know." Kat's theories were rarely comforting.

She told me anyway. "It's because this fucked up city is the fifth circle of Hell. The fifth circle is ruled by anger—and as you know, everyone in Region Five is mad as hell."

Sad truth.

Trident interrupted our little exercise in philosophy. "This is it, Josh. You are clear to move out."

"Roger that."

Trident wanted me to trust him. I'd told him the relationship was moving a little fast, but hell, it's not like I had a choice. He had access to up-to-the-second intelligence summaries prepared by Command's analytical AIs, and to angel-sight from surveillance drones, and to every camera and mic in our squad. All of that gave him a better grasp of the battlefield's dynamics than I could hope to have, despite him being thousands of miles away. I needed his guidance, his input, his oversight. I had to trust him.

I stood, rising easily to my feet despite the weight of my pack, buoyed up by the powerful joints of my exoskeleton. Kat stood too, and together we turned to the squad. *Gen-com*, I thought. My skullcap picked up the request and shifted my audio channel. "Heads up," I said, speaking softly, trusting the com system to boost my voice.

Ten anonymous black visors turned in my direction.

We looked like invaders from space.

The uniform was ordinary gray-brown urban camo, but we were bulked up by body armor, backpacks, and by the arm and leg struts of our exoskeletons, looking like gray external bones. Each of us carried a Harkin Integrated Tactical Rifle—a HITR, naturally—double-triggered to fire both 7.62-millimeter rounds and programmable grenades from the underslung launcher. Wired skullcaps were the external component of our brain-computer interface. Over the skullcap, we wore a helmet with a full-face opaque black visor. The local kids had loved the look of our rigs. To them, we'd been alien heroes, come to Region Five to restore order.

Kids could still dream.

I spoke quickly, quietly. "We're moving out. I'm on point. Follow in your designated order, keep your interval, stick to your projected route, and do not look down." This last was advice to myself. "*Hoo-yah*," I added.

A soft round of responses came back to me over gen-com. "*Hoo-yah*."

The dead stood on the periphery of the living: the lieutenant and two privates, held up by their rigs but slumped—burned and bloodied—heads bowed, faces mercifully hidden behind black visors spider-webbed by impacts. They would move out with us, their exoskeletons operated by the battle AI, judiciously mimicking the pattern of movement it observed in the rest of the squad.

The dead were never left behind. Not the bodies or the gear. It was a matter of honor, sure, but we were also fighting a propaganda war and Command would pancake this building before they allowed the bodies of our brothers and sisters to be mutilated or left to hang in the streets.

I turned back to the abyss, insulated from a direct assault of grief by the constant manipulations of my skullcap. Its activity triggered cascades of neurochemicals intended to keep me focused and alert, in a baseline state of wary intensity. It didn't automatically eliminate fear though, because fear could be a useful emotion in my profession.

I drew a deep breath, all too aware of my racing heart and the tremor in my hands. I reminded myself that if I fucked up, a Kevlar rope would limit my fall. Kat was the anchor, backed up by Porter and Chan. "Don't drop me," I muttered to them.

"Don't get shot," Kat told me.

"And move fast," Trident added. "We took out the last known sniper, but there are always going to be ten more Replacement Parts for every one that falls."

My team, always positive.

I leaned out into the void.

We'd left the stairwell because, two floors up, surveillance showed close to seven hundred civilians waiting to get past an RP checkpoint. They were being identified, searched, and robbed of any useful valuables, before being allowed to cross a sky bridge that led to the relative safety of 21-South. The RPs on that level were vigilant. They had guards set up in the stairwells, and while we could fight our way through, a renewed battle would certainly panic the civilians and lead to unacceptable casualties.

So Command had decided stealth was our best option. We would avoid a fight by climbing unseen up the outside of the tower, until we were past the civilian-occupied floors. Our route was out of sight of the sky bridge, on the opposite side of the building, nestled in an angle of 21-North's postmodern exterior where two semicircular walls intersected.

A rush of a warm wind growled past the rim of my helmet. I refused to look down. Instead, I twisted around, looking up at the side of the building, and as I did, my route appeared as an overlay of reality projected on my visor. I saw two hand holds, indicated by right and left hand prints inside of bright green circles. Clutching the window frame, I grabbed the first hold—a narrow lip of concrete. I set my arm hook over it, and held on with my fingers too, as backup. Then I let go of the window frame and reached for the second hand hold. I did not look down.

I did not *want* to look down.

But I could feel, in the base of my brain, in the back of my neck, just how far I'd fall if the rope broke, if I let go. My hands were shaking. I swear every hair on my body was standing on end as I used my exoskeleton's powered arm struts to haul myself up.

That's when I realized I *had* to look down.

"*Shit*," I whispered off-com. I lowered my gaze, looking for another green circle, knowing it would be there, and it was. This one had a barefoot graphic—and far, far below it was the street. How long would it take me to fall that far? What would I be thinking on the way down?

Then I saw someone run the experiment. A man, dressed in business casuals, took flight from a floor that I guessed to be at least fifteen stories below me. I heard his high-pitched scream. Another man followed after him. I saw it happen this time. I saw the arms that shoved him out a shattered window.

I wrenched my gaze away before they hit. I focused on the projected footprint, jamming the climbing hook of my rig against another lip of concrete, praying it would hold my weight. I boosted myself higher. Found the next foot hold. Released an arm hook and used that to secure the next hand hold.

The hook slipped. It scraped across concrete, sending dried pigeon dung peppering across my visor. I think I stopped breathing. I know my legs were trembling. Not from strain. Physically, the climb was easy because my exoskeleton was doing most of the work. But goddamn, we were thirty-eight stories up, I'd just seen two men plummet to the street, and my skin was puckering. I'd never trained to do this. None of us had. And I hated being this scared. I prayed I'd get shot before I fell.

"Try it again, Josh," Trident said in a voice so calm it irritated the fuck out of me.

I looked again at the next hand hold. It had shifted toward center. I set the hook against it. Got my fingers set. Past gritted teeth, I told Trident, "I'm feeling a little tense." In truth, I was hoping I wouldn't puke. "Maybe you could fix that for me."

I hated having to ask, but what the fuck. Guidance was supposed to take care of my headspace. My skullcap was there to monitor brain activity and to influence it at need. It seemed to me a good time for some artificial rebalancing of my mood chemistry.

Trident spoke slowly, choosing his words. "I don't have a . . . uh, a *precedent* that will allow me to address this situation on my own, but I submitted a request for a prescription."

I didn't ask how long a response would take. It didn't matter, because with or without a fix, I had four floors to climb. So I made myself do it:

Haul up.

Move my right foot.

My left hand.

Left foot.

Right hand.

The rope trailing behind me while I schooled myself to think of nothing but the climb. I moved as fast as I dared, knowing I was an easy target for any sniper who'd evaded the kamikazes, but also concerned for my squad. They were due to follow me, and the sooner the better. If the RPs found them, the door of that office suite would not hold up against a rocket-propelled grenade.

But as much as I wanted to climb that wall with the speed of a circus act, fear made me slow and clumsy. My hands trembled, my armored gloves were wet with sweat, the tiny fans running inside my helmet were not enough to cool the flush that heated my face, and every time I slipped it got worse.

I kept on that way for one and a half floors, and then Trident came to my rescue. "Got your prescription approved," he said.

"Hit me."

He sent the fix to my skullcap, triggering a neurochemical response—and confidence blossomed in my brain. The transition was so extreme I wondered if it was a mistake, an overdose, because Guidance had never let me feel anything that good before. It was a heroic mindset, high, energized, but not manic. No. The opposite: a machinelike focus, and the certainty that I *could* do this without making a mistake.

I sucked in a sharp breath. "I think that's going to work," I told Trident. I looked up, set my grip. Looked down, placed my foot. Repeated that sequence, climbing steadily now. Resisting a subsurface temptation to reflect on what I was doing, or what was being done to me.

Deep down, I knew my prescription confidence wasn't going to last long. There is a limit to how long brain cells can be artificially stimulated before they become exhausted and cease to react. But I let the concern go unexamined, and climbed.

Four floors up, Command had put a rocket through the glass wall of another office suite. The blast had opened the door to the hall, allowing Guidance to send in a palm-sized seeker to scout the floor.

"You got an update for me, Trident?" I asked as I got close.

"The entire floor reads empty, and quiet."

That's what I liked to hear.

I reached the suite and crawled in, onto carpet strewn with broken glass. A glance around showed charred desks and smoldering chairs and artwork and fine ceramics and children's drawings tossed haphazardly against blackened walls. My high drained away, and in just a couple of seconds I returned to real life—that familiar baseline state in which I was wary, alert, and intensely focused on my surroundings. I didn't mind. It's an outlook that's kept me alive through multiple combat missions. Heroic confidence doesn't do that. Soldiers convinced of their invulnerability tend not to last.

I looked toward the door of the suite. It was hanging open on broken hinges. The sight left me feeling exposed. I paused to listen, but the only sounds I heard came from the battle outside. Trident was right. It was quiet up here. There was no hint of the civilian chaos I knew to be unfolding two floors below.

"Okay, Kat," I said. "I'm going to pull up the rope."

"Roger that. We are ready."

I used the single rope to pull up four more, securing them to anchor points already mapped for me in the room. "Okay, let's move."

My soldiers started to climb, four at a time. I lay flat on the glass-strewn floor, looking down, watching their progress. Their gray adaptive camo did a good job of blending with the gray concrete. I listened to their whispers over gen-com as they began the ascent. *Holy fuck*, and *Sweet Jesus*. They sounded impressed, but not scared, because Josh made sure they were high.

Still, "Focus," I reminded them over gen-com. "Move one limb at a time."

The replies came in quiet confidence:

"No worries, Sergeant."

"I'm good."

"I got this."

On-demand confidence. As soon as the first cohort joined me, the second started up. No one hesitated like I had. No one freaked out. They made the ascent quickly, moving from hold to hold as if they'd done this trick a hundred times because belief made it easy, and Guidance was making damn sure they believed.

On the third wave, we hauled up the dead. And then Kat, Lopez, and Fields made the climb.

"Confirm all present," I told Trident.

"Confirmed."

I switched to gen-com. "Next phase commences now."

There were two stairwells inside 21-North's concrete core. The doors to both were closed. That meant I could not send the seeker ahead to investigate. We had to go ourselves.

The closest stairwell was just a few steps away down the darkened hall. The seeker waited for us by the door, hovering at head height, a soft hum emanating from its rotors. I moved up, taking a position to one side of the door, my HITR ready. Raymond took the opposite side. Boldin and Young stacked behind us.

"Ready," I said, and reached out, nudging the door open a crack. Through the gap there came a slice of light and the jumbled voices of a crowd—not close—but not so far away either. The tone was angry, fearful. I couldn't understand the language, but I recognized a shouted threat, a desperate wail. "That's got to be from the checkpoint," Young whispered. A spillover of noise from civilians desperate to cross the sky bridge.

"Agreed." I nudged the door wider and shoved the muzzle of my HITR through the gap, panning it, so the battle AI could use the feed from the muzzle cams to evaluate what was on the other side. As I did, I watched the feed on my visor's display. It showed an empty stairwell lit by emergency LEDs. No debris, no bodies, no booby traps or IEDs in sight.

"Clear to advance," Trident said.

I opened the door wider. The seeker moved first, darting past the door and then zipping down the stairwell—but it descended only a single flight before wheeling around and returning. "Clear below," Trident said. He sent the seeker upstairs next, to reconnoiter hazards above us.

"Young, Raymond." I gestured at them to move toward the lower stairs. "Guard the downstairs approach. Fall in when the squad is past."

I pulled a button camera from my vest pocket, peeled off the backing, and stuck it against the wall, placing it as high as I could reach. Trident would monitor the feed. We'd know if any hostiles passed this point.

"All right," I said, speaking softly over gen-com. "This is it. We should be past the worst of it. All we need to do now is reach the roof. We've got helicopters ready to come in and pick us up. So let's move fast, but keep it quiet. Do not alert the enemy that we are here, and we'll get to enjoy hot showers and home cinema tonight."

I knew the skullcap was working again when I felt another sudden shift in my mood. This time my ready state ramped up, leaving me primed and eager to tackle the last half of our climb. The taut posture of my soldiers reflected a similar mood shift.

"Move out," I said, taking the lead as we set off up the stairs.

This was not the way I'd expected to spend the day.

Fifteen million people. That was the estimated population of the urban maze we called Region Five. For three years, the city's good citizens had worked hard to whittle that number down by killing each other in a brutal civil war. On one side was a dictator who'd accumulated vast wealth and an army of ruthless enforcers. On the other was a revolutionary warlord who'd risen to power on a cult of personality while accumulating a fortune of his own. Reviled by both sides was the tiny educated class—the engineers, administrators, lawyers, skilled contractors and technicians, and the business people, who, together, possessed the thin skin of knowledge every urban complex needs to function. Most had fled during the worst of the hostilities, and what was left of Region Five's infrastructure quickly fell apart.

The threat of mass starvation had proven sufficient to get a peace treaty signed. A few hundred of the essential expats agreed to return, and a coalition of 7,000 peacekeeping troops was promised as "a show of international support." That's how Captain Tardiff had put it, though he'd looked like he had a bad taste in his mouth. "We won't be here long," he'd promised us.

I don't know. We'd been seven weeks in-country. It felt like a long time—but it wasn't time enough for the Coalition to get their act together. We were still operating with half the promised troop numbers. Three thousand soldiers, assigned to occupy a city of fifteen million. The math just wasn't going to work. So we limited our operation to the city center, where people seemed happy to have us around.

But that morning, out on patrol, we all knew something was up. I'd felt the battle AI's anxiety bleeding through my skullcap. We all did.

And then at ten hundred local time, the hammer came down.

In that moment, when I understood we were about to be overrun, I'd felt shock, fear, horror—until a switch in my brain toggled, and I was in battle mode. Maybe it was the skullcap. Maybe it was me. My training. My experience. I'd like to think so, but I don't know.

It didn't really matter. We just had to get the fuck out.

It was a bloody street fight to 21-North. I can see it all in my mind, hear the screams, the gunfire, smell the burn of smoke in the back of my throat, and remember the rage and the grief I'd felt over our dead—but looking back, it feels emotionally distant, as if the memory belongs to someone else.

We wear the skullcaps to ensure it will feel that way. The skullcaps are an interface to keep us focused and on topic, and to distance us from the worst of what we've seen and done.

It's hard sometimes to know what's real.

We moved fast, assured by the seeker that the stairwell above us was clear. Boot plates thumping in soft percussive rhythm, faint hiss of exoskeleton joints, creak of backpacks, low whirr of fans, and the white-noise of breath drawn under duress. My helmet audio should have screened out those noises, but I wanted to hear them. I wanted to focus on them instead of on the distant boom of slamming doors, the screamed threats and the wailing, the occasional crack of gunfire. The tactical AI picked up on that, and allowed it.

We'd climbed only five flights when I felt a tremor in the concrete. It startled me badly. I ducked down against the wall just as the roar of an explosion reached us. My ears popped, and I winced against the pressure in my skull. Lopez was right behind me. He was crouched on the stairs too, with Chan behind him, huddled in a corner of the landing.

Trident spoke over gen-com. "We had four RPs investigating the suite you evacuated. The battle AI triggered the explosives."

Trident had probably watched it happen. That was part of his job: sitting in an air-conditioned office, facing a bank of screens, overseeing the last moments of people he'd helped to target for death. I hoped Command had him wired up, too.

"Roger that," I said.

Recovering my composure, I told Lopez, "You still got a button camera, right? Stick it to the wall. I want to leave more eyes behind us."

We renewed our climb, deploying cameras every few floors.

Our seeker had scouted the stairwell above us, and confirmed it to be clear, but we had no data on who occupied the floors we were passing. That left me feeling like I was in some stupid video game. Every few seconds, I would stride up another flight, turn the corner, see the fire door ahead, the number of the floor painted on it in cool blue. I trained my HITR on each door that I passed, imagining it slamming open to admit a shattering of gunfire from an endless spawn of suicidal characters encroaching from the other side.

Trident interrupted this fantasy with a reality update: "Pursuit is on the way. Enemy seeker has just passed the first wall cam."

I was moving too fast to check my squad map, but I knew Kat would have taken her usual place at the end of our column. I snatched words from between panting breaths. "Kat, that one's yours. Take it out."

"You got it, Sergeant."

"Trident. RPs?"

"Not in sight yet, and I can't hear anything coming."

"Other stairwell, you think?"

"Could be."

We didn't have any devices in place to monitor that route.

I flinched at the harsh report of a three-round burst.

"Seeker down," Kat reported.

"Haul ass," I told her.

The enemy knew now where we were—but the elevators weren't running. They'd have to come up the stairs after us, and I wasn't going to give them a chance to catch up. "Close up any gap in the line," I ordered. "This is a sprint."

Of course it was possible the RPs had personnel already in place above us, positioned out of sight on one of the floors, waiting to launch an ambush.

"Here they come," Trident said. "Enemy now passing the first wall camera. We've got nine . . . no, eleven RPs on your trail. Armed with automatic rifles, a couple of grenade launchers. Manual grenades."

We were way ahead of them.

How long does it take to climb forty stories? We were advancing two or three stairs at a time, each stride powered by our exoskeletons. We still had to work for it, but if no one got in our way, it was only going to take a few minutes to reach the top. "You got our ride incoming?" I asked Trident.

Silence on his side, extending several seconds, long enough to make me worry about a communications issue. I reached the next landing.

"Stairwell's blocked ahead," Trident said. "At least a hundred people—"

"*What?*" I pulled up so abruptly Lopez had to dodge to keep from crashing into me.

"I think they're mostly civilians—"

"What do you mean, you *think?*"

"They knocked down the seeker before I could do a full assessment. I can confirm noncombatants, though. Children. Unarmed women and men. Approach cautiously. Don't shoot unless the AI marks a target."

My LCS was gathering on the stairs below me. On the landing, the fire door told me we were on the seventy-fifth floor. "Why don't I hear them, Trident?" I whispered. "That many civilians, just a few floors up, I should hear voices. Are they alive?"

"*Yes.* Yes, they're alive. They're quiet. They're hushing each other."

That told me they were afraid. They didn't want to be found— but we were going to run right into them, and the RPs would follow.

Trident said, "Intelligence is analyzing the video we were able to get. Using facial recognition to identify them."

Resentment stirred inside me, though at what, I wasn't sure. Maybe at Trident's feigned ignorance as he pretended there was some question about who was hiding on the stairs above. I put an end to that. "They're the expats," I said, starting to climb again. "The technicians, the bureaucrats, the ones who came back to help rebuild this city. The ones the RPs have been throwing out the windows."

The expats had abandoned their country, fled the fighting, only to return in the company of foreign troops. That made them an enemy of the people they'd left behind, right?

"Confirming your guess," Trident said. "But there could be RPs with them."

I snorted. *That* wasn't likely. I reached the seventy-seventh floor. "They're here because they were promised protection, Trident." I knew now why I felt bitter. "Looks like that job falls to us."

So much for an easy run to the roof. I already had three dead soldiers walking behind me up the stairs. How many more of us would become casualties as we waited for a hundred civilians to be evacuated ahead of us?

Trident's voice was soft, apologetic, as he said exactly the opposite of what I expected to hear: "Negative, Josh. Command says you will continue up the stairs to the roof, where you will be evacuated."

"You mean ahead of the civilians?"

To my shock, Captain Tardiff broke in. "The civilians are the responsibility of the Coalition leadership and will be evacuated by them. *My* responsibility is to you and the rest of my people. My orders are to get all of you out safely, with no additional casualties. So you will proceed past the civilians—"

"But Captain Tardiff, sir, the enemy is just a few minutes behind us."

I shouldn't have interrupted him, but his orders weren't making sense to me. That fed my resentment, helped it grow into anger—though I still wasn't sure who or what I should be angry with. The civilians, for getting in my way? The Coalition, for this FUBAR'd operation? The captain, for ordering me to walk away and do nothing to prevent a slaughter? Or myself, because I'd been wishing for an excuse to do exactly that.

The captain sorted it all out nicely: "It's not a matter for debate, Miller. You *will* take your LCS directly to the roof and stand ready to evacuate. Is that understood?"

Yeah, I'm slow, but I do catch on. We'd been brought to Region Five to support the peace process. No one had asked us if we wanted to come. But the expats had volunteered. Now the whole affair was revealed as an empty gesture, a stunt, a performance put on so that afterwards the politicians could shrug and say, *Hey, we tried!*

Sure, the expats had hoped for more—but they should have known better.

Trident monitored the progress of the RPs through the wall cameras we'd left behind. The civilians monitored us through their cell phones.

We saw the first phone tucked into a corner of the stairwell on the eighty-first floor. I knew the local cell system was down, but with peer-to-peer capabilities, the phones could be useful within the building. So I cradled my weapon, and as I passed the phone, I held up a gloved hand and flashed an OK, making sure the American flag on my uniform was visible. I didn't want any resistance when we caught up with them.

Another phone, two floors up, passively observing.

The third phone spoke as I reached it. A woman's voice. I slowed to listen: "We are no threat," she said in crisp English. "Please, there are children with us—"

Some part of my mind wanted to sympathize with her, but what was the point? I couldn't help her. So I cut her off with gruff instructions. "Ma'am, I want to see everyone's hands when I turn the corner. You communicate that to your people. Cooperate, and no one needs to get hurt."

They weren't fools. They did as they were told. I saw them as I approached the eighty-seventh floor. They were packed onto the flight above, mostly men in pale button-down shirts and conservative slacks, watching me between the rails, their hands held shoulder high, palms out. The battle AI assessed the visual feeds received through my helmet cams. It highlighted no weapons.

I noted that they'd left no room to get past them.

Two women, apparently serving as their advance team, waited for me on the landing. One was slim and young, dressed in a dark business suit too hot for this climate, the other middle-aged, a round figure in a flowing brown and beige gown. Both stood with hands up. I guessed the rest of the women and the children were above, on the next flight of stairs which should be the last flight, just below the door to the roof.

The older woman spoke to me in a low, cautious voice. "You are Americans, part of the coalition that invited us here. Will you help us?"

"We're trying to get to the roof, ma'am."

"As are we. We cannot go down. If the revolutionaries find us, they will kill us. We tried to call for help, but the cell system is down. So we resolved to go to the roof, where the Coalition could find us, help us—but the door at the top of the stairs is locked. We can't get through."

I knew I should feel sympathetic. Who wouldn't? We owed these people . . . didn't we? Still, I had my orders. I kept my voice carefully neutral when I assured her, "My people will get the door open, ma'am. But you need to stand aside. Let us pass."

The young woman clutched at her companion's arm, her dark eyes fearful. "You will help us, then? You'll let the Coalition know we are here?"

"They already know you're here, ma'am."

A door slammed somewhere below. I didn't want to question Trident aloud in front of the civilians, so I asked silently, *Trident, how far?* Letting my skullcap pick up the thought and translate it into words that he could hear.

"A few minutes," he assured me. "It's a hard climb and they're getting tired. You've got time to get your LCS to the roof." But then his tone shifted. He didn't sound quite as confident when he said, "They're smashing cameras as they come. I can't be sure of their numbers."

Lopez had moved up beside me. He asked the women, "How many of you are there?"

I raised my hand to cut him off, even as the older woman answered: "One hundred twenty-eight. Thirty-two children."

"Geez, Sergeant. What are we going to do?"

"We're going to get the fucking door open," I snapped, feeling my poisonous resentment on the rise again. From behind my anonymous black visor, I addressed the frightened expats. "This is what I need you to do. I want everyone to move down at least two flights. Keep close to the wall while you do it. Leave the railing clear, so we can get past. We're going to blow the door."

That gave them hope, so they cooperated, opening a lane alongside the railing. I started up, at the same time whispering instructions over gen-com. "Let's move. Quickly. Forget the interval. Stay close. Look for weapons as we go, and push back against any resistance."

Kat protested. "RPs gonna' be here soon, Sergeant. You want me to set up a rear guard, buy some time?"

"Negative." I reached the next flight. The women and children were there. They were moving down while I strode up. They stayed quiet, not wanting to alert any roving RPs, but they watched me, frightened eyes wanting to harbor hope, but unsure if it was a good bet. A little boy reached out, his tiny fingers brushing my exoskeleton's thigh strut as I passed. "We stay together," I told Kat. I knew that once we blew the door, the RPs would come fast and the civilians would panic. "I'm not going to risk a rear guard getting trapped on the wrong side of this mob."

"Yes, Sergeant." She sounded reluctant. She sounded like my conscience.

All of the civilians were behind me when I looked up the last, empty flight of stairs. Another closed steel fire door was at the top. Mounted above the door was an illuminated green sign. I couldn't read it, but the battle AI tagged it with a translation. *Exit.* Yeah? Only if you have the key.

I sent Lopez and Chan ahead to rig the door. Then I eyed my squad map, assuring myself that everyone, even Kat, was obeying orders and coming up behind me. We gathered on the landing, or on the stairs just below. Kat was one level down, last in line. "Civilian coming up fast," she warned.

I heard the quick footsteps, the panting breath. I told Lopez, "Once you get the door open, get outside and take down the antennas. Make it safe for the helicopters."

"Yes, Sergeant."

I leaped down a full flight of stairs to the lower landing, letting the shocks on my rig absorb the impact. My sudden appearance startled the young woman in the business suit who we'd talked to before. The expats crowded behind her, looking frightened, like they wanted to try for the roof again. What would we have to do to hold them back, when panic hit?

The woman's gaze fixed on me, as if she could see my eyes past my visor. She said very softly, "The killers are coming, sir. They're close. A phone picked up their voices."

Over gen-com, Lopez announced, "Fire in the hole."

"Hold up," I told him.

Once the explosives were triggered, the RPs would come after us, berserker style, because that's how they fought—and they'd cut right through the civilians.

I'd known that before, but I had my orders.

"Sergeant?" Lopez asked over gen-com, sounding puzzled.

"These people," I whispered to Trident. "We can't just leave them here."

The woman in the suit looked at me, wide eyed, her worst suspicions confirmed, while Kat backed me up. "It's true, Sergeant. We have a duty."

But Captain Tardiff was speaking again too. "Sergeant Miller, I don't like this anymore than you do, but we are under orders to evacuate. We did what we could, but the mission is over."

My heart was beating fast, my anxiety rising, my conscience white hot. "Captain, it's only ten miles to the airport. That's nothing. You can take the civilians out first. Thirty at a time.

Drop them off, turn the helicopter around. We can hold the roof—"

"*Negative.* There are over seven hundred coalition soldiers to be airlifted out. If you're not on the roof to meet your flight, your LCS goes to the back of the line—and God knows if we'll even have a functional ship by then."

I couldn't believe what I was hearing. "Captain Tardiff, I understand the urgency—"

"Do you? Do you understand what will happen to you if any of you are captured? Do you understand the propaganda cost to future operations? Get your people to the roof *now*, Miller." His tone changed. He wasn't talking to me anymore when he said, "Make it happen, Trident."

Fear. That's what they hit me with. Raw fear from out of nowhere, triggered by some formula that Trident sent to my skull-cap. I teetered on the edge of a panic attack. Cold sweat, racing heart, shallow breathing, and a spine-deep desire to get out, to get away. I'd never felt an artificial load like that before. A skull-cap is supposed to moderate fear, maintain an alert state, cocoon traumatic memories. It was not supposed to take away my good judgment. It was not supposed to make me too afraid to do what was right.

It was abusive to mess with my head like that—and it was *illegal.* I was a US Army soldier and I had rights. I clung to that thought. "Do not *fuck* with my head," I whispered. "Or I am going to take the goddamn skullcap off."

It was a move that would end my career, no question, but in that moment I did not care. I wanted my head clear. The fear eating at me was real, but I knew it wasn't mine and I wasn't going to let it control me. What belonged to me was my resolve that I was not going to let Trident, or the Captain, or the US Army rewrite the core formula of who I was. And that resolve was enough to let me stand firm against Trident's artificial panic.

At the same time, I recognized the truth—I should have seen it before—but Trident must have been in and out of my head ever since we'd discovered the civilians. I felt shame remembering how, just a minute ago, I'd been thinking of them as just an obstacle to be gotten around, not as people with hopes and dreams and core truths of their own.

Kat had known something was wrong with me.

"Get out of my head, Trident," I warned. "Get out *now*."

"*Shit*," Trident whispered. It was the first time I'd heard him swear. But he switched off the artificial fear and brought me back to baseline. He said, "I think you're going to get me fired, Josh."

"You and me, both."

But I was starting to feel like myself again—what I thought of as me—although nothing about our situation was changed. We were in trouble, with an attack by the RPs imminent. "Lopez!" I barked.

"Sergeant?"

"I'm taking Kat. We're going back down. We're going to set up a rearguard. On my word, you blow the door. Make the roof safe, enforce order, and get the civilians out. See that they're evacuated first. I don't care what kind of flack you get. Understood?"

"Roger that, Sergeant."

"Captain Tardiff, you still there?"

"You're going to find yourself up on charges, Miller," he answered. "Assuming you survive."

Was I more determined, because they'd tried to make me panic? It didn't matter. "Command can spin this, Captain. You know they can. Commandeer a helicopter for this building. Prioritize the civilians. You know that's going to make for positive propaganda anyway."

"Goddamn it," he said softly.

I turned to Kat, and off com I asked her, "You with me?"

"Yeah, Sergeant. Let's do this right."

More of my squad spoke up, volunteering for the rear guard. I took only Young and Porter, assigning the rest to help Lopez, or to assist with crowd control.

The civilians squeezed out of the way as we headed down again. They asked no questions. Once we were past them, I whispered to Lopez, "Trigger it."

My helmet blunted the sharp crack of the explosives, but not the fearful cries of the civilians or the chorus of angry shouts and scattered gunfire from below.

Kat leaned over the railing, aiming her HITR straight down. "Movement," she reported.

"Hit 'em," I said. "Grenade."

The Way Home

THE DEMON, LIKE all the others before it, appeared first in the form of a horizontal plume of rust-red grit and vapor. Almost a kilometer away, it moved low to the ground, camouflaged by the waves of hot, shimmering air that rose from the desert hardpan. Lieutenant Matt Whitebird watched it for many seconds before he was sure it was more than a mirage. Then he announced to his squad, "Incoming. Ten o'clock from my position. Only one this time."

But even one was deadly.

Sergeant Carson Cabuto, some six meters to Whitebird's right, huddled against a jut of rock, black as obsidian, a stark contrast to the gray-brown camo of his helmet and combat uniform. "Okay, I see it," Cabuto said. "That's fifty-six minutes since the last one. I was starting to get worried."

"Just starting?"

White teeth flashed in a round face tanned dark by the sun as Cabuto glanced at the lieutenant, his eyes invisible behind black sunglasses. "Now we know the rules, bring it on."

The squad—what was left of it—had taken refuge atop a low plateau, one of several that punched up through the desert plain. Ten-meters high and maybe twenty at its widest point, the plateau's black rock was cracked and fissured, skirted by sharp-edged fragments that had fallen from the walls. The squad had spread out around it, so they could watch the desert in all directions.

Their combat training had neglected to cover a situation in which they were alone in an unmapped desert with no GPS, no air traffic, no vehicles, no goats, no sheep; where the radios worked, but there was no one to talk to; where the enemy emerged from churning dust wielding glittering, lethal swords—but they were learning.

There was no sun above this desert, and no real sky, just a dust-colored glare so bright it was impossible to squint against it for more than a second or two, but though there was no sun, there *was* heat. One hundred twenty-one degrees Fahrenheit according to Whitebird's weather meter. He sucked in the heat with every breath. Belly-down on the black rock, he soaked it in, an exhausting, brutal heat that seeped past his chest armor and the heavy fabric of his combat uniform, heat that got inside his brain, making him think thoughts that never would have entered his mind if he was still in the world. Thoughts like, *If Goodfellow breaks down one more time I'm going to shoot him* and *I'm more than halfway sure we're already dead.*

Whitebird knew that in all likelihood he had simply gone mad.

"This one's coming fast," Sergeant Cabuto warned.

"Roger that."

Madness was not an assumption he could work with. It offered no way out. It demanded that he give up the fight, retreat from the battle, wail at a soulless sky, and pray for a rescue that would never come.

Fuck that.

This was real, for whatever value of real might get defined along the way.

He licked at the salt tang of blood seeping from his cracked lips, wondering if the demons smelled it, or just felt the presence of their souls like an invisible lure, undetectable by any human measure.

Whitebird turned his head, projecting his voice across the rock. "Estimated forty-five seconds until the next dust bunny gets here. Foltz, any more showing up on your side?"

"Not so far, sir!" the specialist shouted back. "But if I spot one, is it mine?"

"This isn't a game, Foltz. Alameri, how about you?"

"Negative, Lieutenant!"

Assurances came back from Fong, Keller, and Cobb that no other demons were in sight.

Last of all, Whitebird turned to Private Goodfellow, down on his belly five meters to the left. The eighteen-year-old was not watching the horizon as he'd been assigned to do. Instead his worried gaze was fixed on the thing of sand and vapor, his gloved fingers clinging so tightly to his assault rifle Whitebird wondered if he intended to use it as a club. "Goodfellow."

The private flinched. He turned to Whitebird. Dust coated the dark skin of his cheeks; behind his protective glasses his eyes were red-rimmed. All the warrior accoutrements—combat uniform, helmet, boots, safety glasses, body armor, backpack, assault rifle, grenades—could not make Goodfellow look like anything but what he was: a scared kid, overwhelmed by the unknown and the unexpected.

"Still with us, Private?"

"Yes, sir," he whispered, not sounding too sure of himself.

"This one is yours."

His brows knit together in abject worry. "Sir, please no, I—"

"You're going." Whitebird didn't want to send Goodfellow. He had more worthy soldiers, but Goodfellow was the weak link and Whitebird didn't want him around. "Stay down," he instructed. "Don't move until I tell you and *do not* use your weapon."

With Goodfellow, the worst-case scenario was all too likely: at some point the kid would panic, and then his friendly fire would be more dangerous than the demons that hunted them. "When I say go, you jump down that ravine. You're only going to have seconds to get to the bottom, so move fast. You got it?"

"Yes, sir."

"Lieutenant," Cabuto warned, "it's here."

Whitebird looked down in time to see the train of dust boil up to the base of the plateau. He could hear the burr of unknown forces swirling within it . . . or maybe that was just the sound of sand rubbing against sand, and maybe the sparks of electricity flaring and dying within the cloud were caused by friction too, or maybe they were generated by magic—he didn't know. He only knew it was a waste of ammo to shoot at the demon while it was in its sand and vapor form. The squad had learned that early. So Whitebird leaned over the edge of the shallow precipice, his M4 carbine aimed at the demon's churning mass, and waited. Sergeant Cabuto did the same.

Seconds passed, and then the skein of sand drew itself upright, a snake raising its head.

"Here we go," Cabuto whispered. "Show yourself, dust bunny."

To Whitebird's shock, the demon's sand form shot up the cliff face. It burst over the top between him and Cabuto, showering them in a storm of grit that crackled and pinged against their helmets and eyewear. Whitebird rolled onto his side, his weapon aimed up as the demon congealed from the cloud.

It came dressed in a gray-brown desert combat uniform, with an M4 carbine clutched in its long, black-clawed fingers.

That was new.

For eight weeks, ever since his unit had transferred to their combat outpost, Whitebird had been haunted by a sense of disaster lurking just out of sight in some unknowable direction. Every night he'd awakened in a rush of panic, sticky with sweat in the aftermath of some monstrous dream. He had told himself it was the altitude, the unrelenting aridity of the high-desert air that made it hard to breathe hemmed in as he was by the bare plywood walls of his little bunkroom.

On most nights he had wound up outside under a blazing firmament of stars, the soft purr of the outpost's generator the only sound in the world—and when the generator cut out, silence enfolded him, silence so deep his brain hallucinated noises and he would imagine he heard a susurration of sand-on-sand, a crackle of electricity, and a haunting, hungry wail that made his hair stand on end—and his heart pound with fear.

He imagined other worlds brushing up against the one he knew.

He never spoke of these imaginings—who would?—and when the generator kicked on again he would go back inside and prepare for the day's assignment.

That day the squad had been patrolling on foot, chasing down numerous reports of insurgents in the district. At the end of a brutally hot afternoon they were returning to the shelter of the outpost—a haphazard collection of plywood buildings surrounded by sand-filled barriers and barbwire, situated at the crown of a low hill. They were five-hundred meters out and Whitebird was looking forward to food and email when a missile came screaming out of the north.

"Get down!" he yelled and dropped to his belly.

He watched the missile hit. It missed the outpost, striking instead the hill beneath it. That hill proved to be made of ancient, weathered, rotten stone. Afterward, Whitebird would conjecture that the slow pressure of a cosmological intrusion had seared and heated and cracked the stone within that hill until it was shot through with dimensional faults and fractures. A blistering weakness, it shattered at the missile's impact, collapsing into roiling clouds of dust and fire . . . and the demons slipped loose—boiling, vaporous plumes sweeping toward the squad with all the deliberate speed and inherent purpose of charging predators.

More than fear, Whitebird felt an instinctive repulsion. He didn't know what was going on. He only knew he didn't want to be touched by it, or caught up in it. Turning to his squad, he screamed at them to run.

Too late.

The land rejected the intrusion. It trembled and heaved and folded in on itself, crushing the demons in the seams of that transition, pinching off their shrieks and wails as day turned to night. Whitebird felt himself falling without ever leaving the ground as if gravity shifted around him . . . and then the sky ignited into an unbearable glare and he was here, his squad with him, prone in the heat and the red dust of a lifeless plain, without a blade of grass or a fly buzzing anywhere around them.

Cast out.

No longer in the world.

———

They had been delivered to a desert plain as flat as an ancient lakebed. Heat shimmers rising from the clay surface bent and blurred the air, limiting clear sight to just a few tens of meters. So they heard the first demon before they saw it—a murmuring of blowing sand though there was no wind, and then a sparking snap of electricity as a train of dust charged into their midst where it congealed into . . .

. . . a glimmering white sword—that was the first thing Whitebird saw, a curved weapon nearly a meter long looking like the tooth of some monstrous *T. rex* or a slaughtered dragon. It was held in long-fingered hands, red-brown like the desert. Behind that primitive weapon was a manlike figure if a man can be seven and a half feet tall with eyes like asymmetrical black fissures slashed into a white-bearded face with red lips around sharp teeth and its tongue a cluster of tentacles glimmering with moisture as it darted in and out, in and out, the creature wearing only a low-slung belt of what looked like human finger bones, with an exaggerated stallion dick dangling flaccid between its legs.

The sword swung, severing Yuen's neck, sending his helmeted head tumbling from his shoulders. Blood fountained just like in the movies. It showered the squad. Screams erupted as everyone fell back, separating themselves from the collapsing body and the long white sword. Whitebird brought his M4 to his shoulder, at the same time dropping to one knee, a move that let him aim up so his rounds wouldn't hit his soldiers who were behind the monster.

He put three quick shots into the demon's chest.

No one knew where the demons came from or what they wanted, but it was now clear that they could learn—and adapt. The creature presently looming above Whitebird was no naked warrior with a sword. It was modernized, weaponized, and far more lethal—assuming it knew how to use the carbine that it held. It hooked a finger over the trigger and started experimenting, firing a string of rounds that hit the rock behind Whitebird. Stone and metal fragments pummeled him as he returned fire, shooting it in the face. Cabuto punched holes in it from behind, shots aimed outside the protection of the armored vest it wore, hitting both shoulder joints and rupturing its neck.

Fire erupted from every wound. Roaring, sinuous streamers of yellow-orange flame, the energy of the demon's existence maybe, bursting into this dimension from some lower world.

The thing arched its back in agony as the fire enveloped it. It shrieked and it shook, but it did not go down. They never did. In the twisted landscape of his exhausted mind, Whitebird was more disturbed by the demon's refusal to collapse than he was by the hellfire, or by the creature's inexplicable appearance out of blowing grit and vapor.

The reality he once knew had been stolen away. The rules were different now.

"Can you see it?" Cabuto shouted over the demon's keening. "Is it opening?"

Whitebird vaulted to his feet, backing away from the searing heat. "Not yet!" But it *would* open. "Goodfellow, get your ass over here!"

"Sir, I—" He backed a step away. "Let Foltz go first. He really wants to go—"

It wasn't a debate. Whitebird had made his decision. He just hoped like Hell—

Ah, fuck that. He needed to cut that phrase right out of his vocabulary. He hoped *to God* he was sending the kid home and not to Hell.

Holding his M4 in one hand, he grabbed Goodfellow's arm with the other and marched him up to the fire while the demon's shrieks faded, as if its voice was retreating into the distance.

Cabuto circled around to watch.

The demon's shape could no longer be seen. The fire that had consumed it became a thin sheet that expanded into a pointed arch seven-and-a-half feet high. As soon as the arch formed it split in the middle, opening along a vertical seam, the fire drawing back until the shimmering flames framed a passage that had been burned through to the world. Whitebird could see through the passage, to home. He knew it was home because he could see the proper color of the sky. He could see figures in the distance in familiar uniforms; he could see vehicles, and helicopters circling the collapsed ruins of the outpost.

Cabuto called it Death's Door.

Whitebird longed to pass through it. So did Cabuto. Everyone wanted a chance to go—except Goodfellow. "Now or never," Whitebird warned him. "You will not be given a second chance."

He shoved the kid hard, and when that failed to convince him, he brought his weapon to his shoulder and trained the muzzle on Goodfellow's face. "Go now, or die here."

For a second, Goodfellow was too shocked to react—but then he stepped through, a moment before the fire burned itself out. When Death's Door closed, he was on the other side.

Whitebird intended to get everyone out, but it was a slow, dangerous game, and it had taken time to learn the basic rules: that a door only opened if they killed a demon, and then only one soldier could pass through.

No one knew why.

No one knew who had made the rules: God or the Devil or an ancient magician or random chance. It didn't matter. "We know how to get home. That's all that matters."

Whitebird knew—they all knew—that the longer any of them stayed in that place, the more likely they were to die there. The demons might kill them or worse, the demons might stop trying to kill them. If the demons didn't come hunting them, if there were no demons to kill, there would be no passage back and whoever was left behind would die of thirst.

So in his mind Whitebird weighed the merits of each of his soldiers. He balanced the potential of their unknowable futures against the immediate needs of the squad, and he developed a list in his head that prioritized their lives.

"Keller!"

"Yes, sir," she answered from her position on the opposite side of the little plateau. Specialist Trish Keller, who had a year-old daughter and no support from the dad.

"You're going home next, Keller. Be ready."

"Lieutenant, who goes after Keller?" Foltz wanted to know.

Foltz was a good, determined soldier, but not a selfless one. He'd been putting himself forward at every opportunity, pushing hard to be the next to go home—but Sergeant Cabuto didn't approve of his lobbying.

"Knock off the chatter, Foltz! Keep your eyes on the desert. The lieutenant will let you know when it's your turn."

Whitebird squinted at the glassy haze of heat shimmers rising above the dust, going over again in his head the evacuation list he'd developed. Foltz was going to be disappointed, because after Keller he planned to send Private Bridget Cobb, who was an only child. Then Private Ben Fong, who would make an excellent non-com if he lived long enough. Only after that would he let Omar Foltz go, and after him, Private Jordana Alameri, who was basically a fuck up and didn't have much of a future to go home to. Once his soldiers had all made it back, then Sergeant Cabuto would be willing to go.

It was a tentative schedule, subject to revision. Whitebird considered moving Cabuto up the list, ordering him to follow Keller. He didn't want to have to get by without the sergeant, but Cabuto had a wife and three kids. Or maybe he should send Alameri next. After this tour of Hell's suburb she might be ready to walk the straight and narrow.

There was only one position on the list that Whitebird was sure about and that was his own. He would go last, which meant that for some unknown interval of time, a few seconds or forever, he would be here alone—and what that would be like?

It didn't bear thinking on.

After Yuen died and Whitebird killed the first demon, Death's Door had opened for the first time. Foltz had been nearby. He'd seen through to the world and had tossed a rock into the passage to test the way—but the rock bounced back.

Specialist Jacobs had a different idea. "Let's try something from *our* world." He moved in close to the searing fire, tossed a cartridge—and it passed through. The squad pressed in around him despite the heat, watching the glittering cartridge shrink with distance and then silently strike the ground on the other side, bouncing and skipping across the familiar gray grit of the desert they used to patrol.

There was a nervous catch in Jacob's voice when he announced, "You know what? I'm going home." Then he stepped through.

Whitebird had been badly startled. He'd grabbed at Jacobs, tried to catch him, to pull him back out of harm's way but Jacobs was already on the other side, a distant figure seen in utter clarity as he turned to look back at them. His mouth moved with words Whitebird could not hear as he gestured emphatically for them to follow—but Whitebird could not follow. The passage pushed at his mind and he could not move his limbs in any way that would take him through it.

"Foltz, *go!*" he ordered, and Foltz was willing.

He pushed past the lieutenant and tried to push on into the passage, but it was closed to him too. When he realized it, he turned on Whitebird in an explosion of frustration. "Goddamnit, Lieutenant! What the fuck is going on? Is this some kind of crazy experiment? Yuen is fucking *dead*. What the Hell did you get us into?"

Jacobs was still looking back at them from the other side when Death's Door closed.

What did you get us into?

Whitebird had no answer for that or any of the other questions the squad lobbed at him:

What is this place?
Why are we here?
Is this Hell?

"I don't know!"

They clustered around him, Cobb and Goodfellow weeping, Keller praying quietly, her folded hands pressed to her forehead, the rest clutching their M4s, their gazes flitting from him, to each other, to the heat-blurred horizon—scared, suspicious, angry.

Whitebird forced himself to use a matter-of-fact voice: "I don't know what happened. I don't know why we're here, but we *are* going back. Sergeant Cabuto!"

The sergeant stepped up, stern, determined. "Sir!"

"Set up a perimeter guard."

"Roger that, sir."

Foltz still had questions. "I don't get it, sir. Why the Hell did Jacobs get to go back? He did go back, didn't he? It looked like he went back."

"He went back," Whitebird confirmed. He was not going to allow doubt on that—it was all they had to hold onto—but the question that really mattered was, could they do it again? Could they send someone else back?

He put Keller to work inventorying their supplies and then he helped get Yuen's head and body wrapped up in an emergency blanket. When that was done, he conferenced with Cabuto. "If it happens again, we need to be ready."

"Agreed, sir."

They pulled Private Lono aside, selecting him because he was their strongest man.

Whitebird asked him, "If the chance comes, are you willing to try it? To follow Jacobs?"

"Roger that, sir. I sure as fuck don't want to die here."

Whitebird nodded. "I want you to carry Yuen's body with you when you go. We'll follow if we can."

Out on the open plain Whitebird felt too vulnerable, so he directed the squad to make for the nearest plateau. They would take turns carrying Yuen's body.

They'd been walking only a few minutes when the second demon came. The soldiers out front started shooting when it was still churning sand. That drove it back, but only briefly. It charged in again, congealing into existence only inches from Fong, who fired his M4 point-blank at its belly and then fled as fire erupted.

The passage back to the world opened just like the first time, and Lono escaped with Yuen's body. But though Keller tried to follow, she could not.

The next demon came just as they reached the rocks and it got LaBerge.

After that, two demons came together. One was killed. Fernandez used its death to return to the world with LaBerge over his shoulder. After he left, Cobb got all weepy, claiming she'd seen LaBerge's soul seeping through the passage—"Like a glowing light cleaner and brighter than daylight"—which convinced Whitebird that she was full of shit because there was nothing clean and bright about LaBerge's soul.

But that didn't mean he'd deserved to die here, halfway to Hell, with his head cut off by a lunatic demon.

They spread out once again around the top of the small plateau, waiting for another demon to appear. Five minutes crept past, and then ten before Cabuto spotted a sand plume, far out on the desert and barely discernible above the heat shimmers. It churned up against the wall of another low plateau a kilometer and a half away, and disappeared.

Fong spotted another, but it too failed to come after them.

It had been six hours since the squad dropped out of the world but there was no sign of nightfall in this place and the heat remained constant. They'd been low on water from the start. Soon it would be gone and then they'd have only a few hours before they succumbed to dehydration. They needed to find more demons before then.

Whitebird turned to catch Cabuto's eye. "We're moving out. The dust bunnies didn't have any trouble finding us on the plain."

Cabuto turned to look again at the next plateau, a black island rising from the shimmering red-brown flat. "We saw one disappear over there."

Whitebird nodded. It was as good a direction as any.

———————

They made their way down from the rocks and then set off across the hard clay surface. Every footfall sent a puff of fine red dust into the still air. Sweat leaped off their skin, evaporating as soon as it formed. Whitebird sipped at his remaining water, but the relief it brought was wiped out by the next breath of hot, dry air.

They stayed ten meters apart. Whitebird and Foltz marched in front, Cobb, Alameri, and Fong formed a second rank, and Cabuto and Keller held the rear, keeping watch behind them.

They couldn't see far. Hot air rose in shimmering columns, reflecting distant plateaus while hiding what was really there so that again, like the first time, they heard the demon before they saw it. "Three o'clock!" Whitebird called out, turning toward a faint rustling white noise.

"I can hear another," Cabuto warned. "Five o'clock."

"Fucking *two* dust bunnies?" Alameri grumbled. "Again?"

"Two tickets home," Whitebird reminded her. "Fall back if they materialize between us—and stay alert for more."

"I see it!" Foltz shouted. "Three o'clock!"

"Fall back!"

"Incoming from behind!" Cabuto warned.

The two plumes of sand and vapor churned past their outer ranks, converging in the middle where Cobb had been standing. She tried to get away. She plunged right through one of the sand plumes, but the other curled around to cut her off. Both demons transformed. Giant figures, they stood back-to-back, dressed in desert camo and armed with carbines. Cobb was caught between them as gunfire erupted from all sides.

Whitebird dove for the ground. Bullets chewed through the hot air as demon howls broke out, competing with the racket of the weapons. The demons had been hit. Whitebird rolled, coming up on one knee to see the two creatures on fire, their weapons burning and useless in their hands—with Cobb sprawled and bloody on the ground between them.

"Cease fire!" he screamed. "Cease fire!"

The shooting ended and Whitebird charged toward the two

flaming figures. As he did, he saw Foltz move in the corner of his eye. "Foltz! Help me get Cobb!"

"But sir—"

"*Now!*" He crouched beside Cobb. Her jaw was shattered. Blood soaked her right arm and thigh. Grabbing her pack strap, he dragged her away from the fire.

Goddamn. Goddamn.

The demons couldn't have shot her where she'd been standing. "Foltz!"

Whitebird looked up to see Keller, Fong, Foltz, and Alameri, all waiting near the flames.

"Keller goes next!" Whitebird ordered. He strode into their midst, grabbed Foltz, shoved him away, shoved Alameri. "And you, Fong, go."

Foltz and Alameri looked mutinous, so Whitebird kept his finger just above the trigger of his M4 and watched them until Keller and Fong were gone.

Foltz cursed into the quiet that descended. "Goddamn *shit*. Why the fuck do I have to stay here? Why? We are going to fucking *die* here."

From somewhere behind Whitebird, Cabuto spoke. "Lieutenant, Cobb's not going to make it."

"I know that."

"I can't get a heartbeat. We've lost her." And then, "*Holy shit.* Lieutenant, you have to see this."

Whitebird turned.

Cabuto was backing away from Cobb as a black shadow, utterly dark, seeped up from the ground beneath her body. It spread out to surround her, and as it did, Cobb sank into it, her shattered corpse dropping slowly away—into some place worse than this one?

"Don't let her go."

"She's dead, sir."

What did that mean, here? LaBerge had died here. Yuen had died. This had not happened to them.

Whitebird rushed to Cobb's side, went to his knees and grabbed for her, but though she was only inches away, he couldn't touch her. A twist of geometry had placed her out of reach as she lay cradled in darkness, her eyes hidden behind sunglasses, but with the mangled flesh and shattered bone and broken teeth of her jaw exposed.

He didn't exactly see it happen. He couldn't point to the moment, but the pliant geometry that held her stretched and shifted and she was suddenly away, lying on rocky soil among tufts of grass with a moon rising over sharp peaks, spilling a yellow light.

Whitebird knew the place. "That's home. That's right by the outpost." He looked up at Cabuto. "Go. Follow her. Follow her through."

Pale dust frosted Cabuto's dark face. "No, sir. We've got two soldiers who need to go ahead of me, sir."

"*Goddamn it,*" Whitebird whispered. "I want *you* to go."

"Not before them, Lieutenant. No fucking way."

Whitebird stood up, furious. Cabuto was worth more than Foltz and Alameri together. He had a wife and kids. Arguing, though, would only waste the chance.

"Foltz!"

Foltz was still steps away, cursing his luck, but Whitebird discovered that Private Alameri had come quietly to his side. She looked up at him from behind her dark sunglasses. He nodded. "*Go.* And don't waste your fucking life."

No hesitation. As Foltz came charging up, she stepped into the shadow and then she was standing on the other side, standing beside the body, an infinite distance away but still close enough that he could see her as she turned, looking up at the three of them gazing down at her. Then searing desert light infiltrated the shadow, destroying it, leaving only hardpan covered in red dust.

"What the fuck just happened?" Foltz screamed, probing at the ground with the butt of his weapon and then hammering at it. "Why did that happen?"

"Death's Door," Cabuto said.

Foltz turned on him. "It didn't happen when Yuen died! Or LaBerge! What was different this time?"

"Leave it!" Whitebird snapped. He already knew what made this death different. "It just fucking happened. You are going to make it home, Foltz."

"Yeah? Alive or dead?"

"Alive if you can hold yourself together. What happened to Cobb doesn't need to happen again. It was an accident."

Whitebird regretted the words as soon as they were out, because they pointed Foltz to the truth.

He backed a step away, eyeing Whitebird with a guarded expression. "The demons didn't kill her, did they? *We* killed her."

"Friendly fire," Cabuto affirmed as he turned in a slow circle, eyeing the terrain.

"But it's not going to happen again," Whitebird added.

Foltz nodded, though he was thinking hard.

Thinking the same thing Whitebird was thinking: that Death's Door opened every time they took a life . . . and not just a demon's life. They knew that now, but it was a poisonous knowledge.

"We're in this together," Whitebird emphasized.

Foltz nodded again, though he did not seem convinced.

They went on, deciding that it was more likely another demon would notice them if they kept moving. Or maybe more than one would come. There might even be three. Three would be enough to get them all home and then Whitebird wouldn't have to stay here alone.

He'd kept his fear locked up for hours, but they were close to the end now and his dread of what that meant was rising up to choke him. Foltz would get to go home next, and then Cabuto. Whitebird would make sure of that. It was his duty. He swore to himself he would make it happen.

Then only he would be left behind, left here, alone.

And if the demons killed him, then what? There was no one to take his body back. What would become of his soul?

He wasn't sure he believed in a soul, but he worried over it anyway.

A faint susurration reached his ears, barely audible over the crunch of their boots, the creak of their packs. He stopped and turned, scanning the plain—and this time he saw the demons at a distance, reflected in the heat shimmers so that their plumes of dust appeared elevated above the ground. One snaked toward them from two o'clock and another from four o'clock, two came from behind, and a fifth raced in from their left.

"Ah, *fuck*," Cabuto swore.

Whitebird said, "*Run.*"

Their packs banged against their backs as they sprinted for the rocks. Cabuto took the lead with Foltz on his heels. Whitebird followed. If they could get behind the fallen boulders with their backs against the black cliff, then they could make a defense, hold the demons at bay, reduce their numbers . . .

But they were already too late.

More than an hour ago they'd watched a plume of sand and vapor wander the plain before disappearing into these rocks. That demon was still there, waiting for them. Dressed in desert camo with an M4 carbine in its black-clawed hands, it crouched behind the shelter of a massive, angular boulder lying like a black prism on the ground. They were fifteen meters away when it started shooting.

The first shots went wild. Then a burst struck Cabuto in his chest armor, knocking him over backward. Foltz caught a round in his hip. It spun him, dropping him ass-first to the ground. Whitebird jumped over him, jumped sideways, pulled a grenade from his vest, and hurled it behind the rock as a bullet chewed past his helmet.

He dove for the ground. The grenade went off.

The explosion blasted a cloud of dust into the air and shook the cliff hard enough that an avalanche of sharp stones dislodged, tumbling down with a roar. The body of the demon ignited on the edge of the debris.

Foltz saw it and heaved himself up in an act of will that somehow got him to his feet. Under the incandescent light of the false sky, the blood that soaked his hip blazed red. He took a step and his leg gave out. He sat down hard again. "Goddamn it! Goddamn it, Whitebird, you got to help me!"

Cabuto, a few meters behind Foltz, had recovered enough to make it to his hands and knees. He rocked back to a kneeling position, his weapon aimed at the oncoming assault. The storm front of demons was a hundred meters out, five plumes that blended into one, bearing down on them with a low whisper of sand on sand, punctuated by the sharp crack of arcing electricity.

"Help me!" Foltz screamed.

Whitebird ran past him, ran past Cabuto, and lobbed another grenade, heaving it as far as he could in the direction of the oncoming cloud. It went off ahead of the churning sand, with no effect that he could see. He looked back over his shoulder.

The burning demon swayed like a balloon afloat on hot air, its feet just brushing the hardpan as flames spread over it in a blazing sheet: the prelude to Death's Door opening. Foltz was trying to drag himself toward it, but for him, it was too far.

So for the last time, Whitebird mentally updated the order of his evacuation list. "On your feet, Sergeant," he said, rejoining Cabuto. "This one's yours. You can make it if you run. Now, *move!*"

Cabuto didn't. He scowled past dark sunglasses while keeping his weapon trained on the oncoming cloud. "Take Foltz, sir!"

"Goddamn it, there's no time! Get on your feet and go!"

Foltz had stopped his slow crawl. He twisted around, his M4 gripped in two hands. Past the blood-smeared lenses of his safety glasses, Whitebird saw fury and a sense of betrayal in his gaze. "Foltz," he said, trying to reassure, "I'm staying with you."

But a decision had already crystallized in Foltz's eyes. A calculation born of logic and desperation: there was still a way for him to go home.

The demon storm was eighty meters out when Foltz raised his weapon, training the muzzle of his M4 on Whitebird, and on Cabuto, who was still kneeling with his back turned.

Whitebird screamed "*No!*"—but it was already a meaningless protest, an empty aftermath to a decision made and acted upon. Deep in the pragmatic layers of his battle-trained mind, he'd concluded a calculation of his own. His conscience continued to wrestle with the choice even as his own weapon fired in a drawn-out peal of hammering thunder, dumping slugs into the midline of Foltz's chest armor, stitching a straight line to his throat, through his face, shattering his glasses and his skull. His weapon flew out of his hands, tumbling, caught in a shower of blood.

Cabuto lunged to his feet. He spun around, eyes wide with horror, his mouth a round orifice of shock as he held his M4 tucked against his shoulder, contemplating Whitebird over its sights.

Whitebird shook his head, gesturing with his own gun at a black shadow seeping up through the desert floor, enfolding Foltz's body. "*Go.*" Already, the body was subsiding into darkness. "Go, Sergeant. Follow him home."

"You killed him!" Cabuto screamed. "Why? Just to buy a way out?"

Whitebird answered, saying what Cabuto needed to hear: "He was aiming to kill *you*. Us. We were his passage out of here. You saw him before. You know what he was thinking. I had no choice." But that wasn't the whole truth. "I fucked up and called it wrong. He was never a hero—and I let him think he could be left behind."

Cabuto looked like he wanted to argue more, but what was left to argue?

"Go *now!*" Whitebird shouted, knowing that neither of them—no one who had been in that place—would ever really leave.

The sergeant's gaze shifted to the burning demon, transformed now into an arch of flame framing a transient passage back to the world. "You better get your ass in gear, Lieutenant. You better fucking *run!*"

Cabuto turned and stumbled into the shadow, dropping out of Whitebird's sight.

The swirling sand storm was almost on him when Whitebird took off, sprinting for the fire. The demon-driven sand swept past him and then spun around, encircling him to block his way but he plunged through it, the grains hammering in tiny, painful pricks against his cheeks and pinging against his sunglasses, his helmet, his clothes. Demon figures resolved out of the red-tinged chaos, some armed with white swords and others with guns.

Whitebird started shooting. He emptied his magazine at half-seen shapes, until he felt the fire's searing heat radiant against his face. Only then did he look at it, and within the encircling arch of flame he saw familiar stars spangling the moon-washed night sky of home—a step away or an infinite distance, he didn't know.

In the dusty air above his head the whistling passage of a demon's white blade sounded, descending on him.

He dove.

The Last Good Man

The following chapters are excerpted from the novel, The Last Good Man. *The setting is the near future, somewhere in the Middle East. A private military company has launched a hostage rescue operation. Along with standard weaponry, the PMC is equipped with robotics ranging from insect-sized surveillance devices to unmanned fighter jets—but success is never assured.*

One Chance

Miles isn't surprised when gunfire erupts downstairs. He's been expecting some kind of operation ever since he saw the mosquito drone, but, "*Shit,*" he whispers to himself. "Why did they wait until Noël was dead?"

Then he's up, military training taking over. There isn't enough light in the stinking little room to see, but he's memorized the place, the positions of his companions. "Ryan, you up?"

"Right next to you."

Miles feels a hand on his shoulder. Ryan is alert and ready to act; he saw the mosquito drone too.

"Get in the corner," Miles says, giving him a gentle shove. "Face the wall. Cover your head."

"What the hell is going on?" Dano demands in his thick Brazilian accent.

"We're hoping it's a rescue."

"What rescue? What do you mean? How do you know it's a rescue?"

Miles hears doors open. Shouts, footsteps. Decides against debate. Groping in the dark, he finds Dano, grabs the front of his shirt—"Get over here"—hauls him into the corner. "Get down. Cover your head. Protect your eyes."

He huddles with Ryan and Dano. Flinches as a flurry of shots erupts. A loud bang. Running footsteps. New voices. American voices. Dano tries to get up. Miles won't let him.

"Stay back from the door!" someone shouts. A woman's practiced command voice. "We're getting you out of here but we have to blow the lock. In five!"

"We're ready!" Miles shouts.

"Might want to cover your ears," the woman suggests.

The gunfire downstairs has ceased. Distant shouts and a car alarm's faraway bleat mingle with the heartbeat thump of her retreating footsteps.

Boom!

Miles winces, feeling like he's been punched in both ears. Then he's up again, hauling Dano with him, knowing Ryan will follow. He still can't see a damn thing. He gropes for the door anyway, finds it ajar, pulls it wider. A tiny red light flicks on in the hall outside. It casts shape into the world, defines the hallway, but it does no more than suggest the presence of a camouflaged figure behind the light. She is a conception, a sketch of a soldier drawn to confuse the eye. Definition exists only in her gloved hands, the screen of her MARC visor, and in the solid mass of the Kieffer-Obermark resting in the crook of her arm.

True, looking back at him, finds herself caught in a moment of weird dissociation. Her visor shows her a light-amplified view of this stranger, Miles Dushane. He's dressed in a shapeless tunic and stained trousers, face gaunt, beard tangled, his hair dirty and disheveled. She does not know him, has never met him before. And yet between one heartbeat and the next it feels to her as if both time and space are folding around him, bringing forward a more familiar presence.

Haven't I dreamed this? she asks herself. *Of opening this locked door?*

Yes. And though it is Miles Dushane who looks back at her from beyond the doorway, she sees through him into a parallel past, to another prisoner, a young man not so different from him, also slated for brutal execution.

Her heart beats again. Time restarts. The past falls away. It is forever beyond reach, and still, a connection remains. It leaves a pressure behind her eyes, a tightness in her chest as she resolves that what happened before will not happen again. *Not this time.* Miles is not her son, but he is someone's child, a good man from all that she's heard, and it consoles her to be here tonight, to ensure that he, at least, survives.

She speaks in a voice purposely brusque, businesslike, no reflection at all of that space between heartbeats. "What's your condition?" she asks. "Any significant injuries? Broken bones? Anything that will prevent you from getting down the stairs?"

Miles too uses brusque words, but his voice is husky with emotion. "No," he tells her. "We're all ambulatory." He watches the red light move closer. It takes him a few seconds to realize she is holding it out to him. He accepts it by instinct.

"Step out here," she instructs him. "You first. The others to follow one at a time. I need to pat you down."

"Yes, ma'am." He does as she says, stepping into the hall. Only then does he notice a second soldier, a big man waiting halfway down the hall, keeping close watch on the proceedings, ready to bring his weapon into play. Beyond him, four men are on the floor, bound and therefore presumably alive. Miles holds his arms out. The woman runs her hands over him, quickly, professionally, stooping to check his legs and crotch.

Behind him, in the stinking cell, Dano protests. "I don't understand. Who is this woman? How do we know we can trust her?"

Miles answers with an impatience verging on anger. "I know she's not fucking Hussam and that's good enough for me."

"You're clear," the soldier tells him. "Who's next? Let's move."

"Go on, Dano," Ryan growls from the dark. "Or get the fuck out of my way."

Dano stumbles into sight, off balance like he's been pushed.

Miles catches his arm, pulls him into the hallway, and tells him, "Stand still."

He stands frozen, staring at the men on the floor while the soldier pats him down. She finds nothing, turns to Ryan, and repeats the procedure.

"All right," she says when she's done. "My name is True Brighton. I'm here with an American PMC called Requisite Operations. If you cooperate and move fast, we will get you out of here. But it's all or nothing. There won't be a second chance. If you want to live, follow Jameson." She gestures at the second soldier. "*Move out.*"

She doesn't seek their agreement. She doesn't need it. This is their one chance at freedom. Ryan understands that. When Jameson starts down the hall, Ryan totters after him, unsteady for lack of exercise but determined. Miles keeps his grip on Dano's arm and follows.

But Dano still isn't sure. Shock and confusion piled on top of months of stress have left him adrift, focused on the wrong things, on things he can't control. After two steps he plants his feet and demands, "What about Fatima? Fatima Atwan? Dr. Atwan is my colleague. She is a prisoner too. We can't leave her behind."

Miles doesn't have an answer. This isn't his operation. For all he knows, Fatima is dead. "Right now, Dano, you need to shut up and do as you're told. I swear if you slow me down I will leave you behind."

"I just—"

"Dr. Atwan is downstairs," True says, crowding behind them. "She's coming with us. Now move."

Dano gives in. He allows Miles to steer him. The little red light picks out the men on the floor, picks out the face of Abu Khamani glaring at them as they stumble past. *Aloha, asshole*, Miles thinks, but he's too disciplined to say it aloud—or maybe he's too superstitious. They're not home yet.

His light finds the top of the stairs. He directs the beam down. The dim red glow wraps around an indistinct figure. "Ryan, is that you?"

Ryan confirms it. "Right here, pal."

Miles follows with Dano, the red light revealing one step, then the next. He can't see Jameson. Wrapped in darkness and camouflage, the soldier has become invisible.

But though Miles can't see much, he hears things. Male voices. A hard percussion of footsteps. The throaty rush of wind.

He reaches a landing. From somewhere below comes a woman's wailing wordless cry, one that shifts suddenly to a screaming protest in American-accented English. *"No, no, you don't understand. It won't help. It's too late."*

Dano is energized by that voice. "Fatima!" he yells in response. He picks up his pace, rushing Miles to the bottom of the stairs. "Fatima, where are you?"

Miles tightens his grip. "Leave it to the professionals," he warns.

True peels off at the bottom of the stairs, leaving the three hostages to make their own way to the door.

"Lincoln."

"Here."

"Going to pick up a few souvenirs."

"Do it. But be at the door in ninety seconds."

"Roger that."

She returns to the office that she and Jameson cleared on the way in. The door hangs open, its latch broken from when Jameson kicked it. She slips off her pack, digs out two radio-frequency shielded collection bags, and loads them with the obvious storage media: a laptop, a tablet, drives, sticks. That's all she can take. She seals the bags.

"Lincoln."

"Here."

"I'm going to leave a kamikaze crab."

He's silent for almost five seconds. Then he says, "All right. Do it. The structure of the house should support it."

She shrugs the pack back on, slings her KO over her shoulder, and with the two bags in hand, heads for the door. It's been a few minutes since she checked in with Juliet, who was posted to the courtyard. Time to catch up.

"Juliet," she says over comms. "What's your status?"

"Prepped and ready. I've got the canopy sliced open and our bots collected."

"You got all the mayflies?"

"Roger that. Recovered all four."

Good. True is concerned about the legality of the mayflies. The neurotoxin they deliver might be considered chemical warfare. Best not to leave evidence behind.

Miles follows the beam of his red light around furnishings set up like obstacles in a large room. Ahead is an open doorway with a thin slice of dusty night sky visible beyond. Jameson waits there. Ryan heads for the door but the soldier says, "Hold up. Stand on the side. Keep the door clear. We exit last."

Miles moves up, stands behind Jameson. From outside he hears the muted roar of powerful engines. A distant jet? And another aircraft, closer.

Boom!

He drops into a crouch, pulling Dano down with him as searing light flickers in the slice of night sky. A courtyard and two parked trucks are briefly revealed, along with a canopy, sliced open, loose edges rippling in the wind.

"That was us," Jameson says. "Just clearing the skies of cameras."

Miles stands up again, shaking. Ryan is right beside him, breathing in labored gasps. "Hey," Miles says. "You okay?"

"Ask me in ten."

"Right."

A clatter of motion draws his attention back to the house's interior. A shadowy tide of soldiers, more sensed than seen, flows from a hallway to the left of the stairs. As they reach the door, glints from their visors and red sparks reflected from his little light give them vague definition. Miles counts four of them and realizes they are carrying a body. He gets only a glimpse before they're out the door, but that's enough for a mental snapshot. The body is confined in a canvas bag zipped up to the chin; a black hood covers its head. The sight makes the hair on the back of his neck stand on end. He is sure the body is Hussam's.

All or nothing, he thinks. Either they get out of here in the next few minutes or every one of them is dead. He grits his teeth and waits for the signal to move out.

Aircraft noise gets louder, deafening, as a helicopter comes in. No navigation lights. No spotlight. It hovers over the courtyard, rotor wash blasting dust in through the open doorway.

Miles leans over to get a better look at the operation, but it's too dark to see what's going on. All he can make out are shadows and glints. Then an oblong object rises into the slice of open sky, its shape silhouetted against charcoal clouds. Hussam's corpse. It's lifted over the wall as the unseen helicopter roars away.

With the engine noise in retreat, Miles hears something else, something closer: a woman breathing in tiny, high-pitched gasps. She sounds as if she's just inches away. Cautiously, he raises his light.

Dano turns to look too. "*Fatima*," he whispers.

She is dressed in a thin white shift. A broad Velcro restraining strap secures her arms against her body. A soldier stands behind her, gloved hands on her shoulders. Fatima wears no veil, no hijab. Her black hair hangs loose and wild, and in the red light her eyes have the appearance of unnatural black pits, haunted, in a face that is waxy and drawn.

"Dushane, are you ready?" True Brighton asks him.

He startles at the question, having lost track of her. He turns, finds her beside him, and answers, "Yes, ma'am. Are we getting the fuck out of here now, ma'am?"

"Roger that. We are crossing the courtyard and exiting through the gate, into the street. You will get your people into the back of the waiting truck. Understood?"

"Absolutely, ma'am."

"Switch off your light."

"Yes, ma'am."

"Let's go."

Miles can't see a damn thing as they move out across the court-yard. All he can do is follow the sound of the soldiers ahead of him while keeping a hand on Ryan's shoulder and a grip on Dano's arm. Grit under his bare feet and the occasional thorn make him wince, but he doesn't slow down. Ahead he hears shouts and the ripping thunder of over-accelerating gasoline engines racing toward their position. It sounds like this escape attempt is going to run straight into the enemy's arms. But there's no going back.

The shooting starts as they reach the gate. He sees distant muzzle flashes like sideways candles. Hears bullets buzzing down the street, tumbling against the walls. Answering fire erupts, deafening in its proximity. The attackers fall back.

There is no moon, and there are no houselights to be seen any-where along the street. Blowing dust shrouds all but the brightest stars. He can see a waiting truck only by the dim red light that spills from its open doors. It's a double-cab pickup with a high clearance and a rigid canopy enclosing the cargo bed. One of the soldiers opens the tailgate doors. "Get inside! Strap into a harness if you can. If not, fucking hold on."

Ryan doesn't hesitate; he scrambles right in. Miles pushes Dano after him and then crawls in behind.

It's a good-sized space. There are side windows in the canopy and a skylight four and a half feet above the cargo bed. A thick mat covers the bed and the walls.

Ryan raps his knuckles against the canopy. "Solid," he announces. "Fucker's armored."

Canvas seats and harnesses are anchored to the sidewalls. Nets stretched across the ceiling hold gear. Miles can see these details because red light from the cab wells through an intervening win-dow, providing a baseline illumination. There's not enough light for him to be sure, but it looks like one net holds spare magazines and another has packs of what could be C-4. One thing he is certain about is a collection of helmets. He pops that net and pulls them out.

Ryan has moved all the way in, taking a seat closest to the cab. He pulls on a harness. Dano straps in next to him.

"Put these on," Miles says, handing them helmets. Then he straps in too, facing them, shoulder against the cab window.

Six soldiers climb in after them, vague shapes crowding in the near dark. The cargo bed fills with the heat of bodies and the smell of fresh sweat. The tailgate doors slam shut, muting the sound of gunfire. Facemasks come off, helmets go on.

In the cab, more soldiers. Miles watches them through the window. He recognizes Jameson riding shotgun. A leaner guy already strapped in behind the wheel. Two more in the backseat, wrestling with Fatima. She is struggling in her restraints, resisting their efforts to get her strapped safely in. Does she even understand this is a rescue? Or in her mind is she being kidnapped again?

Harnesses are secured. Doors close. The engine revs and the truck surges forward. Somewhere behind them, a muffled explosion. Outside, the shooting starts up again.

A side window close to Miles is shoved open. He ducks, not wanting to catch a stray bullet. Faint red highlights let him identify a KO in the hands of the soldier beside him. The weapon is aimed out the window, but the soldier isn't shooting. No one in the truck is shooting. The gunfire outside fades into intermittent firecracker pops, barely audible over the rush of air past the open window.

The window gets slammed shut.

A hearty masculine voice rises above the road noise. "Listen up, friends. My name is Rohan and this is a Requisite Operations mission. Things are going to get ugly in the next few minutes, but don't worry. The air force is looking out for us, and we *will* get you home. So hold on and don't get in the way."

Leaving Town

Khalid is behind the wheel of the DF-21, a rugged, lightly armored truck that the QRF is relying on to get them out of Tadmur. True is squeezed into the backseat. She's behind Jameson, who's up front riding shotgun because he's too damn big to sit anywhere else. Fatima is next to her, with Chris on the far side.

True is braced against the DF-21's acceleration, holding her KO in a one-handed grip, her other hand poised above the switch that will lower the window if she needs to shoot. She has used her weapon only once over the course of the mission. She hopes she won't have to use it again. A street battle would guarantee civilian casualties. Not something they want.

They'll engage only if they are trapped and have no choice.

She leans forward to look at the dash display, where there's a feed from a rearview camera. She can see muzzle flash and she gets a glimpse of what might be a pursuing truck before Khalid wrenches the DF-21 around a corner.

Damn.

True had hoped to stave off pursuit. When they pulled out, she triggered the kamikazes. The devices, designed to deliver small controlled explosions, would have taken out the electronics in the downstairs office and disabled both trucks in the compound without damaging any neighboring homes.

But Hussam was the head of the Al-Furat Coalition. He had allies and soldiers in the surrounding neighborhood. No way to sabotage all their vehicles.

Fatima too is watching the rearview display, her expression fixed except for her lips which move as she speaks too softly to be heard over the road noise. A prayer, maybe.

Chris had summarized her condition over comms as he worked with True to get her strapped into a safety harness.

"No gross physical injuries," he said, speaking just loud enough for the mic to pick up his voice, but not so loud that Fatima could hear. "But he's fucked with her head. When we came in, she tried to protect him. I don't think she understands why we're here."

"She's in shock," True said.

"Yeah. And unpredictable. That's why she's in restraints. You need to talk her down."

It isn't a good time for talking. True grabs a handhold, bracing herself as Khalid whips the DF-21 hard around a traffic circle. He's riding an adrenaline high, racing to get them out into open desert. "We got fucking Hussam!" he shouts, his voice amplified over comms. "I can't believe it. We got the self-righteous bastard. And we got him *alive.*"

Rohan answers over comms, annoyingly matter-of-fact, given the circumstances: "Bounty pays either way."

True turns to look in the back. The light-amplifying property of her visor reveals the tense faces of the three rescued hostages, and beyond them Juliet, Nate, Nasir, Felice, and Rohan, all strapped into canvas seats and swaying in unison as Khalid uses speed to smooth the bumps in the road. Rohan notices her gaze and flashes a thumbs-up. Shadows hide his smile but she knows it's there.

Gunfire rips overhead. Her first instinct is to duck. Her second is to trigger the window to open so she can return fire. The thick glass drops out of sight, the roaring of jet engines pours in on the dusty air. Lincoln yells over comms: "No threat! Reseal the truck. That was just RQ-3 discouraging a rooftop shooter."

"*Fuck,*" True whispers, all too aware of her booming heart. She triggers the window to close again. Jameson and Chris close their windows too.

RQ-3 is one of a trio of Hai-Lin UF-29s—unmanned fighters—that make up ReqOps' air force. Lincoln has assigned all three to this mission to provide an escort for the DF-21 and for Blackbird as it carries Hussam away.

True calls up Blackbird's status on her display. The Kobrin 900-s reports itself at twelve hundred feet and still climbing. Hussam is suspended beneath the little autonomous helicopter, in a Kevlar cargo pouch at the end of a tether. If Blackbird is shot down, Hussam will go down with it. Under no circumstances will he be released alive back into the wild.

RQ-3 continues to shadow the DF-21. True hears its engine even past the armored sanctity of the cab and the blast of its air conditioning. She watches the buildings flash past, but there is no more gunfire. No resistance.

Abruptly they are past the last compound and into open desert. The DF-21's headlights are off. Khalid is no longer wearing his AltWrld visor. He's got a MARC instead, to help him see in the dark. True doesn't envy his task. She can hardly see the road past the streamers of sand that skitter across it—but it's easy to see where the road is going, because its path is marked in the distance by the fierce silhouettes of the burned-out tanks they passed on the way in.

This desert: ravaged by war and not much left to fight over. There's petroleum in the ground still, though it's not worth what it used to be. It's not worth the hell this region has become. Here, now, the fighting is an end in itself, a way of life, and that cold fact is one reason why PMCs like ReqOps exist.

"Couple of technicals behind us," Rohan says over comms.

True leans forward to look again at the dash display. The feed from the rearview camera is a kind of night vision, but shifted to display in dull red. It shows two small pickup trucks pursuing them out of Tadmur. Both are running with lights off. Machine guns are mounted in their cargo beds.

Lincoln assures the team, "We're on it."

The command post's wall monitor displays a continuously updated three-dimensional map of the desert outside Tadmur. It lets Lincoln track the shifting positions of ReqOps' equipment: the squadron of three Hai-Lin fighters, Blackbird, and the DF-21 racing up the highway. Also, a civilian convoy moving south. And of course the enemy, currently represented by two technicals speeding past Tadmur's outlying neighborhood.

"Targets acquired," Renata announces in a stern voice, operating from behind VR goggles. "Authorization?"

"Stand by," Lincoln tells her. "Let's give them a few more seconds to clear the town."

Hayden, at his desk in front of the monitor, drags RQ-3's feed from the screen's periphery, depositing it beside the map. It shows only desert and mountains as the UAV circles, getting in position for a strike. Onboard AIs pilot the Hai-Lins, but it's Renata who commands the squadron through the twitching, tapping motion of her fingers inside their black-lace gloves. She provides instruction, oversight, and authorization for the use of weapons.

"Okay," Lincoln tells her. "You're authorized. Take the shot at your discretion."

"Acknowledging authorization."

Hayden looks back, wide-eyed in excitement. He's never seen the Hai-Lins used in combat before. None of them have. This is the first time the UAVs will fire weapons in a live operation. Lincoln feels a touch against his arm and glances down to find Tamara beside him, come to watch.

RQ-3 completes its turn. The technicals are dead ahead.

Renata says, "Missiles away."

Even as she speaks, their leased surveillance drone, cruising high above the action, issues a red alert.

On the dash screen, True glimpses a missile streaking in from the southern sky, almost too fast to see, and then sequential explosions erupt: billowing fireballs that swallow the two technicals, spitting out hard pieces, gun turrets and engine blocks that tumble into the night. She feels the concussion in her ears, in her bones.

The DF-21 jumps as Khalid leans harder on the accelerator.

"Take it easy," Chris snaps. "We're clear. No one left back there."

Lincoln says, "Premature assessment, Chris. We are *not* clear. Three bogies inbound from the southeast. Silhouetting as Arkinson XOs. No transponders."

"*Fuck*," Chris whispers in high-definition audio.

True's grip tightens on the armrest, tightens around the stock of her KO as she pushes back against lurching fear. None of their pre-mission intelligence indicated Al-Furat possessed Arkinsons—cheap and disposable jet-powered UAVs with a per-unit cost of just over five million American. They're designed to carry a payload of four slim Tau Hammer missiles—self-guided hunters that can obliterate a lightly armed ground vehicle like the DF-21 as easily as RQ-3 took out the technicals and the soldiers who rode in them. The absence of transponders means there's no telling who the Arkinsons belong to, though it's a damn good indication they're not friendlies.

The worst part: there's nothing anyone in the DF-21 can do

to defend themselves. No need to look farther than the scattered debris of the technicals behind them or the looming silhouettes of the burned-out tanks ahead for evidence of that. It's on Renata to serve as their champion, wielding her squadron of Hai-Lins. True is grateful the Hai-Lins are out there, but it's a hard truth that her life and the lives of everyone in the DF-21 rely on the battle skills of machines, of competing AIs, to determine if they ever get home.

Lincoln's first move is to simplify the battle space.

He opens a voice link to the Kobrin 900-s carrying Hussam. "Blackbird," he orders, "move out. West along the highway, maximum speed while maintaining current elevation."

"You want an escort with that?" Renata asks from behind her VR goggles.

"Negative." Blackbird is slow compared to the oncoming Arkinsons and it's only lightly armed, making it as vulnerable as the DF-21, but it's not carrying ReqOps personnel, so it's not a priority. Hussam El-Hashem is its only cargo, and while Lincoln would like to deliver him alive, it isn't necessary. The bounty will still pay and it'll cover the loss of the helicopter. He tells Renata, "Focus defensive operations on our people. Set up for autonomous defense, standard protocol, and hold."

"Roger that, boss," she responds. "Three on three."

Lincoln's gaze fixes on the three-dimensional map. "Tamara, check known armaments for the Iraqi government."

"Already on it, Lincoln," she answers. "And . . . negative. Arkinsons are not part of the Iraqi arsenal. Probably a private registration. Checking area PMCs."

Lincoln's jaw sets. He got into the business of soldiering when he was eighteen, in part because it was what he knew, what he'd grown up with. But he also wanted to serve. Serve his country, serve the greater good, using the skills he was blessed with to do it. The QRF is a new phase in that tradition of service. His people are out there at the risk of their lives. It is his duty to support them to the extent of his abilities and the limit of his credit line. If it comes to a dogfight, ReqOps could lose a Hai-Lin, maybe more than one, escalating the cost of the operation. But if so, he'll make it up in other business. He'll take the chance, because he is all in. That's the promise he makes to his people. No halfway measures.

Without waiting for Tamara's search results, he issues his next order. "Renata, initiate defensive response."

The rules of private combat are mostly unwritten but well understood among companies that regularly operate in the TEZ. A neutral PMC would not send equipment into the field to interfere with a third-party action. So the Arkinsons' presence in their area of operation marks them as enemy combatants, freeing Lincoln to take defensive actions, confident that he will not incur sanctions from the US government or ReqOps' allied contractors.

In all circumstances, right action demands that the welfare of civilian bystanders be taken into account, and as a practical matter, any PMC concerned with maintaining a viable reputation, one that allows it to operate openly, would strive to avoid collateral damage and loss of life. But in the real world, war is a messy business—which is why there is a thriving regional company specializing in the negotiation of financial compensation for incidental deaths, injuries, and the destruction of property.

But on the desert highway there are no innocent civilians to be caught in the line of fire and the only property involved is the already war-torn road.

"I don't care who the Arkinsons belong to," Lincoln says. "Neutralize them. Do not let them get off a shot."

"Roger that. Initiating autonomous defense, standard protocol, targeting Bogie-1, Bogie-2, Bogie-3. Weapons are active."

With the standard protocol in effect, the squadron AIs will operate on an instruction set written to minimize collateral property damage and avoid all civilian casualties. Excessive safeguards, tonight. "Correction," Lincoln intones. "Friend or foe."

"Confirming friend-or-foe protocol," Renata echoes in a crisp, emotionless voice. The squadron AIs will no longer have to calculate the probability of collateral damage, a change that will speed up their response time. As Renata cedes control, her hands go still.

The map shows the trio of Hai-Lins peeling apart. Lincoln doesn't know what their next move will be. Neither does Renata. Unless the Arkinsons withdraw, they are about to witness a dogfight between AIs. The Hai-Lins are technically superior, but they're not fully loaded. RQ-3 has already spent missiles against the technicals. And the AIs that fly the squadron have never before engaged in actual aerial combat. Up until now, all their battle experience has been in simulations. Their training will meet reality tonight.

True doesn't see the unmanned jets engaging over the desert, but she hears them despite the DF-21's insulation, despite its armor, the rumble of its engine, the rattling of its frame as Khalid leans on the accelerator, racing west to escape the battle. But there's no way he can outrun combat aircraft. The drone fighters scream in the night, nearer, farther. Loud enough to shake the stars.

She braces with one hand on the back of Jameson's seat, thinking of Alex and how angry he'll be if it ends here for her, if she doesn't make it home.

The DF-21 shoots over a slight rise. It goes briefly airborne, then comes down hard, skidding across a patch of sand. True feels the jolt in her spine as she's held down by the bruising grip of her harness. Beside her, Fatima gasps. Angry yells erupt in back.

It takes True a second to get her harness to loosen up enough that she can move again. When she does, she turns to check Fatima, who sits hunched in her restraints, loose hair hiding her face. True looks next into the cargo bed. If anyone back there got bounced around, it could mean a broken neck, a broken back. But everyone is strapped in, strapped down. Saved by their restraints but furious all the same.

True looks to the front again and shouts over the road noise. "Khalid, you in a hurry?"

"We're okay, Mama," he yells back. He doesn't slow down. "I just want to make sure we get home!" Fear lurks beneath the bravado in his voice.

"I want to get home too," Jameson warns him from an arm's reach away in the shotgun seat. "If you roll us, kid, I swear I'm gonna break your neck."

Fatima raises her head. She cannot raise her hands—her restraints prevent it—so she shakes her head to get the lank hair off her face. Her oily cheeks reflect the console's red gleam. Red glints give an unholy aura to her eyes.

"He *will* come," she warns in a despairing voice. "You cannot win. He will burn us all. He will."

"Fatima," True says, not quite touching her. When Fatima turns, True tries to meet that hopeless gaze, despite the jerky jumpy motion of the racing truck. She tries to plant hope, saying, "He wants you to believe that, but *I* think we can win. And this much I know for sure: Hussam will be a prisoner of US forces by dawn, or he will be dead. For him there is no escape."

Fatima opens her mouth as if to argue, but whatever words she intends are crushed by the thunder of a jet passing directly above them. Animal instinct kicks in and everyone ducks. Even Khalid, behind the wheel.

But no autocannon fires. No missile hits them. True grasps the reason first: "Must have been one of ours. If an Arkinson passed that close, we'd be dead."

"*Fuck!*" Khalid swears as he straightens in his seat. His fingers hold the wheel in a bony grip while on his cheeks, rivulets of sweat trap the red light.

Rohan's laugh belts out over comms. Pumped up, riding an adrenaline high he says, "Take it easy, Khalid! There's no way we can outrun this fight. We live or die by the grace of our squadron AIs."

"*Truth,*" True whispers.

Ahead of them, electric-white light bursts across the desert. Briefly, it illuminates nearly a mile of empty road. Inside the truck the chatter dies. They listen: to road noise, to the throaty bellow of the engine, the dopplered roar of jets. Waiting to learn who won.

The concussive rumble of an explosion rolls in, background soundtrack to Lincoln's stern voice. "One enemy aircraft down. The other two are in retreat. The sky is ours."

Cheers ring out in both cab and cargo bed, but True does not take part. "What's Blackbird's status?" she asks, voice cutting through the celebration.

Lincoln says: "Blackbird has overrun the rendezvous. Heading back now. Otherwise nominal."

True's fingers twitch as she calls up their position on her display. It's twelve K to the rendezvous and the next phase of this mission.

"All the pieces in place?" Chris wants to know.

"On the way," Lincoln assures him. "We delayed the transport helicopter pending the outcome of the air war, but it's inbound now. We'll be back on schedule soon."

"And the merchandise?" Chris asks.

"Blackbird's camera shows it still kicking."

Wrapped in the backseat's shadows, True allows herself a small private smile. Machines dominate the battlefield, but it took human soldiers to snatch a bad guy from his bedroom and recover four captives from their prison.

It's a moment of contentment that doesn't last.

"Shit," Khalid says. "I see lights. Ahead of us. Goddamn army's worth."

—◦◦◦—

The Last Good Man
is available in print, ebook, and audio editions.

Books by Linda Nagata

NEAR-FUTURE SCIENCE FICTION
Pacific Storm
The Last Good Man
Limit of Vision
Tech-Heaven
The Red Trilogy:
    The Red: First Light
    The Trials
    Going Dark

FAR-FUTURE SCIENCE FICTION
Inverted Frontier Series:
    Edges
    Silver
    Needle
The Nanotech Succession:
    Tech-Heaven (prequel)
    The Bohr Maker
    Deception Well
    Vast
Memory
Skye-Object 3270-a (young adult/middle grade)

FANTASY NOVELS
The Wild Trilogy:
    The Snow Chanter
    The Long War
    Days of Storm
Stories of the Puzzle Lands Duology:
    The Dread Hammer
    Hepen the Watcher

SHORT FICTION COLLECTIONS
Light And Shadow: Eight Short Stories
Goddesses & Other Stories

CPSIA information can be obtained
at www.ICGtesting.com
Printed in the USA
BVHW040254150622
639748BV00003B/10